Stalking
The
Stalker

LAURA HAWKS

Laura Hawks

Soaring on Wings
One Story at a Time

FURTHER BOOKS BY LAURA HAWKS:

Words For Warriors II: A Word Search Book
The Balconies of New Orleans

YA Paranormal Mystery:
Gumshoe and the Mysterious Mushrooms

(Please note: The following are adult books)

Demon Trilogy: Demon's Kiss
Demon's Dream
Demon's Web

Spirit Walker's Thrillers:
Shifter's Hope
Shifter's Pride
Shifter's Journey

Ghost and the Grimoire

Fractured Fairytales:
Snow White & The 7 Cannibals

Valley View Mysteries:
Flaming Retribution
Stalking the Stalker

DEDICATION

I would like to dedicate this book to my mother, who is always and forever in my heart. She was the encouragement I sometimes needed. She was the person who was proud of every accomplishment I had. She was my supporter in every part of my life and she was my best friend. She will always be missed.

I would also like to dedicate this book to my mother's sisters, the last of which passed May 2018. My mother was one of eight children and many had a strong influence on my life. I will miss the feeling of family they always instilled within me and the love and safety I was always surrounded by.

I hope all of you take the time to appreciate your family, whether born to or chosen, for they are everything in the universe.

ACKNOWLEDGMENTS

I'd like to thank Nancy Knoell, who has reminded me there are lights that shine brightly and who always has a smile. Although I don't get to see her much, her presence is very dear to me.

Also, I'd like to thank my PA Ashleigh Turner who has been a life saver in helping me get organized better so I can continue to do what I like the most.. tell stories.

Thank you to all of my fans. Each of your notes, emails and posts have been very much appreciated.

After you finish reading this book, I hope you will also take the time to let me know your thoughts. Platforms to contact me are located in the back of the book under About The Author. I would also greatly appreciate it if you would leave a review on Amazon and/or Goodreads.

Thank you again for your patronage and friendship.

Prologue

Mackenzie Harper tucked her long brown hair behind her ear and pulled out her phone. She was concerned when her mother didn't show up for church, which quickly turned to worry when Louise Harper still hadn't put in an appearance for their weekly brunch date. Her mother was slightly anal and would've at least called her twenty-three-year-old daughter if she were feeling too unwell to attend services or their get-together. It was one of the few standing appointments they had, making sure they wouldn't get so busy with their own lives they lost touch. Mackenzie knew Louise looked forward to their time together too much to have missed it.

Pulling out her phone, she dialed her mom for the tenth time. Still no answer. Quickly, she made her way to her car while dialing the police department.

"Valley View Police, operator 115. How can I

help you today?" The young woman's calm voice gave Mackenzie a sense of helpfulness.

Maybe she was being silly, but she'd rather be over-cautious than ignore the possibility her mother needed help. "I'd like to request a well-being check for my mom."

"Can you tell me what happened?"

"My mom and I have a standing date for church and then brunch at The Hungry Hamster and she didn't show at either. Nor has she called me, and she's not answering her phone. She lives alone. I'm on my way over, but I'd appreciate it if the police could check it out since I'm about twenty minutes away. In case she's fallen and can't get up or something." Although her mother was only 48, she'd lived a hard life and appeared older than she actually was. Arthritis was setting in her knees and she had a bad back. If she'd fallen, she'd need assistance getting back up.

"Okay, ma'am. What's the address?"

"1325 Calloway Drive. It's a house."

"And her name, please."

"Louise. Louise Harper."

"Alright, I'll send the officers there and let them know you'll meet them as they cannot enter the home without proper cause if there's no answer and they don't see anything amiss."

"Fair enough. I'm on my way there now. Thank you."

Although Mackenzie wanted to speed through the streets of Valley View, she knew getting a ticket—or worse: into an accident—wouldn't be prudent, but that didn't stop her heart from racing as she swerved around a few vehicles that seemed as if they were going slower than the speed limit.

As she approached the house, Mackenzie could see two police vehicles parked outside and the officers standing near them. She parked a bit haphazardly in her anxiousness to check on her mother. She just knew, deep down, something was seriously wrong.

"Hi. I'm Mackenzie Harper. I'm the one who called. Did you find my mother?"

"Ma'am." One of the officers, wearing the

nametag Simon, stepped up to greet her. "There was no answer and the drapes are closed so we couldn't see inside."

"I have a spare key." Mackenzie started to rummage through the metal keys hanging from her leather keychain, her hands beginning to shake. It took her a moment to find the right one and she started to head towards the door with her hand outstretched.

Officer Simon gently touched her hand. "Would you like us to check it out first?"

Mackenzie nodded, grateful. She was frightened over what she might find and wasn't quite ready to face the possibility of her mother being seriously hurt.

"Wait here."

Mackenzie nodded and crossed her arms, as if fighting an unseen chill despite the warmth of the day. After a few moments, she couldn't stand the unknown any longer and slowly approached the front door, entering the foyer. She'd not taken but a few steps into the house when Officer Simon approached her. "I'm sorry, Ms. Harper. I'm going to need you to step outside."

"Why? What's wrong? Where's my mom?" Panic caused her voice to raise as she tried to push past the officer and see for herself, her heart dropping into her stomach with her nerves.

"Let's go outside. I'm sorry, there isn't anything you can do for her now."

"What? What do you mean?" Mackenzie heard the words, but the intent wasn't registering in her brain.

"I'm sorry to inform you, your mother is deceased."

"She's dead? How is that possible? I just talked to her yesterday. She's in good health. She's not that old."

"Ma'am, I regret to say she was killed."

"Killed? Killed!? Who? How? I don't understand!" Mackenzie was stunned, her mind unable to comprehend what she'd just been told. "No. You must be mistaken." As grief began to set in, her heart felt like it was in a vise, slowly tightening within her chest, and water pooled in her eyes before they overflowed, beginning a tumultuous stream down her cheeks.

"Why don't we go to the police station so we can talk? I'm going to need your help to figure out who wanted your mother dead."

"Yeah. Sure. I guess." She was in complete shock, willing to be led around like a sheep as she reeled from the news. "How? Please tell me how?"

As Officer Mark Simon walked her back out the front door, he sighed softly. Breaking news like this to a family member was one of the hardest parts of his job and he detested it more than anything. It'd be a detective who'd take over the investigation, but until then, she had the right to know something. The details she'd have to get from the detective assigned to the case. "She was stabbed."

Mackenzie turned away from him and threw up in the bushes beside the house.

Chapter One

Two weeks before the murder:

Kendall Roberts looked at her reflection in the mirror. She couldn't believe this day had finally arrived. And though she was extremely happy, she was also a bit melancholy. After all, her mother wasn't here to see her walk down the aisle to a man Kendall still couldn't believe loved her so much. "If you don't love yourself, how can you ever expect others to?" her mother often asked. But Kendall almost threw everything away because she didn't believe in herself enough to think she deserved someone like Skye Falcon. Skye had the body of an Adonis with the most engaging turquoise eyes she'd ever encountered without contacts. She paled in comparison to him, with her ebony hair and hazel-green eyes. She was certainly not the type of person anyone would dream about, at least not until Skye walked, or rather danced, into her life.

She'd met Skye just over sixteen months ago at a male dance club called the Cock-a-Doodle. She'd gone for inspiration for her romance novels. Since the death of her mother, just months before, Kendall had done all she could do to motivate herself to move on. Prior to that, she'd spent almost all her time caring for the woman who was as much her best friend as she was her mother. Relationships, dating, hell, even sex went to the wayside. Her mother was all that mattered, especially once she was diagnosed with breast cancer. Kendall couldn't do enough for the woman who gave her life. Yet, as a romance novelist, she'd almost forgotten what a man felt like when he moved against her fingers, and if she was going to write about it, she needed some reminders, even if they were only visual.

Chuckling slightly to herself, she couldn't help but admit how terrified she was of him when he seemed to search her out as she hid in the back of the busy club by herself. Truth was, she'd no intentions of ever seeing him again, if not for almost being run over as she left the building that night. As they both escaped the maniac chasing after them, they watched in horror as the club exploded. Skye became determined not to let her out of his sight until the monster trying to kill her was captured. Since he was also a volunteer fireman, he was able to get constant status reports of police progress about the case.

In the end, she ended up moving in with him at his instance after her home was also destroyed, and though it took a bit of convincing, he proved to her how beautiful and wanted she was by him. Today, they were making it official in front of their friends. Neither had any family left, but they had each other and she was okay with that.

Kendall had been so lost in her own thoughts she never heard her best friend and matron of honor, Louise Harper, come into the room. Kendall met Louise about a year ago at a Moraine Valley village picnic to honor first responders. Louise had known Skye for a few years and was thrilled to meet the woman who had captured his heart. Realizing Kendall lost her mother, Louise immediately took her under her wing, growing close in the process. Kendall wasn't sure what she'd have done without the woman's sage advice over the last couple of years.

"Okay. Tink is all set with Cassie, and everyone else is waiting. Are you ready for this? It's almost time." Louise moved towards her with a tiara veil in her hands, placed it on Kendall's head and used a couple of bobby pins to keep it in place.

"Believe it or not, yes, I'm ready. I'm not even that nervous or scared."

"That just means you found the right guy. Such a shame he doesn't have a brother for me." Louise fanned out the veil and stood back. "Perfect."

Kendall smiled back at their reflections in the mirror. "Yeah. I'm very lucky, despite meeting him under such auspicious circumstances. As for him having a brother, you're still married."

"Separated. And I filed for divorce just last week." Louise immediately waved away the look of sympathy she saw come into Kendall's eyes. "You're going to have a much better marriage than I ever did. Skye took the time to get to know you first. Lots of guys don't seem to bother now."

Kendall turned around and took Louise's hands. "Actually, I never thought I was good enough or pretty enough for him. He spent most of the first couple of months together convincing me otherwise."

"See, that's what I mean. He's a really special guy and you're very lucky."

Kendall grinned. "Yes. Yes, I am." *Even better, I don't have to go to male strip clubs to get inspiration for my novels. Skye keeps me well occupied and willing to experiment to make my stories more entertaining and authentic.* She had the feeling their honeymoon would give her plenty of inspiration for her next novel. "I thought you had someone new in your life too. You've not been as available the last couple of months, and didn't I hear you mention about some new guy in your life?"

Louise's cheeks flamed so red the color spread to her ears, visible with her brown hair pulled into a coiffeur atop her head. "Yeah. I met him online several months ago and we've been talking daily for hours on end." Louise would never admit he was part of a role-playing game online or that he now played her mate. She lived for him and loved him, and though she'd never met the person behind the computer screen, she didn't care. He'd given her the attention she'd always craved, even if it was only through the airwaves of the internet.

"So, you've not actually met him in person?"

"Once I did. A very long time ago, but he doesn't remember." Actually, she'd only met the avatar used by him, not her role-play partner.

"And? What does he look like?"

"Handsome. Not as much as Skye, but much better than Al." Al being her soon-to-be ex-husband.

"And he's kind?"

"Very much so, Kendall. He's attentive, sweet, romantic. When my divorce is final, we're going to be very happy together."

"Did you bring him to the wedding?"

"No. You'll meet him soon. He'll be in town in a couple of days."

"Oh! What a shame he couldn't come sooner and make the wedding. I'd've loved to have met him."

"You'll meet him soon enough. I promise." She fixed Kendall's dress one last time. "Ready? Can't keep your sexy hunk waiting too much longer."

Kendall laughed and nodded, leading the way out of the dressing room.

The music started to play. Cassie walked down the aisle holding Kendall's feline companion dressed in a turquoise dress. Which, of course, drew tons of attention and giggles from the crowd at the formally dressed Tinkerbell. The little furball was part of Kendall's only family and Skye knew what the cat meant to Kendall, insisting Tinkerbell be a part of the ceremony.

Louise then walked down the aisle, followed by Kendall, who just glowed with happiness.

Although Louise was thrilled for Kendall, she really wished she were in front of her computer with Lucas. His hazel eyes and strong, athletic body made her own tingle. Thoughts of their writing together made her blood flow hot and she hated having this time apart from him, even if this was an important day in her dear friend's life.

Thankfully, the ceremony was over relatively quickly, so Louise could pull out her cell phone and hop onto Facebook to see if Lucas had responded to her last post. Her heart raced at what he might have written, and she was very disappointed when there was no response yet.

"Louise? Where are you? We need you for the pictures."

Hearing Kendall call out to her, Louise put her phone away and rushed to the area where the photos were being taken, all the while wondering when Lucas was going to respond.

Louise kept looking at her phone throughout the reception, and by the time dinner was completed, she finally had a response from him. Grinning from ear to ear, she sat at the table, posting back to his response. His reply was almost immediate, Louise continued to write on the thread from her phone. She almost jumped when her daughter, Mackenzie, was pulling out a chair next to her and sitting down. "Are you on that phone again? Gee, Mom, you're worse than most of the kids I know. They can at least put their phones aside for a couple of hours. And don't give me that look. I've seen you checking it every chance you've had."

Louise frowned at her. She'd had her at a young age. Louise didn't look old enough to have a full-grown daughter who lived at the other end of town, in the village of Moraine Valley.

"I don't spend that much time on Facebook.."

Mackenzie snorted. "You practically live on it. I'm actually amazed you get off it long enough to go to church and meet me for brunch. Or even do normal stuff, like shop and cook."

"You're starting to sound like your father."

"Maybe he has a point with regards to this. You virtually live on Facebook. What is so important all the time that you can't enjoy what's happening in the real world?"

"I do enjoy what's happening here. I just enjoy being in that world a bit more."

Mackenzie looked astounded. "I can't believe you said that! No wonder Dad left you. I hate you for this." She shoved her chair back and stormed off.

Louise watched her until she was out of the room. Maybe she should pay more attention to those in the world around her and not so much on Lucas and Facebook. However, she'd been so unhappy with Al as her husband that delving into the fantasy world of role-play had been her only solace with a loveless marriage. Maybe she did push Al away, but she wasn't sorry she did. Actually, she felt relieved to know she didn't have to placate him any longer. She was free. Lonely, yes, but free from pretending to care for a man who held no interest to her and, for the most part, annoyed her by his very existence. Lucas became her refuge. Lucas gave her an escape into a better world: one of her imagination and creation. In that world, she was perfect, beautiful, young and adventurous, with a perfect body and perfect skin that would attract men by the dozen—and she had her pick. Lucas was perfect. He challenged her mind, connected with her soul. He was everything she'd ever wanted and everything she dreamed about. If only Mackenzie could understand how trapped Louise felt all these years, or how she found something in a fantasy world she could only wish for otherwise.

Pulling up a news article she'd saved on her phone, she read the announcement again. *Tyler Channing comes to Valley View to star in the new play* Tell Me About It. *Written by Kendall Roberts and directed by Byron Cassiday, the play will run at the Pixard Theater from May 31 until September 1. Tickets on sale at the box office.*

Tyler Channing was the face Lucas used for his character on Facebook. Louise'd met Tyler ages ago, when he was first starting out as an actor. She'd even had the opportunity to spend alone time with him. When Lucas was contemplating whose famous picture to use for his character's profile, she strongly recommended Tyler Channing and he willingly agreed. Louise knew Lucas did it only to please her, but even a gesture so small was more than Al ever did for her. Now Tyler was coming to Valley View and she'd have the chance to meet him again. Yes, she knew Tyler was different from the avatar Lucas used, but it didn't matter. Her heart still fluttered uncontrollably at the thought of seeing Tyler once again. Besides, maybe it was just her imagination, but with Lucas needing to be offline next week—he stated it was because he was going on vacation—a small part of her felt that vacation would be taking place right here in Valley View.

"How about a dance?"

Louise looked up from her phone, surprised to see Al by her side, his hand out to her. It took her a moment to remember Al was friends with the groom Skye. At first she was going to refuse, but what the hell? It was a wedding reception and she'd already upset her daughter. Maybe if Mackenzie saw her doing something other than be on her phone, she'd forgive her. Louise truly loved her daughter and wished they spent more time together. At least they had a standing date on Sundays, a day

Lucas worked in the morning and couldn't be online, giving her the free time to not worry about missing his posts.

"Sure. Why not?" She gave him her hand and he led her out onto the dance floor. Taking Louise into his arms, they slowly moved across the dance floor. After a few moments of silence, Al took a deep breath. "Mac is pretty upset."

"I know."

"You realize it's because of your addiction to the computer that we're separated."

"You know I filed for divorce, right? You got the papers?"

"Yeah. I got 'em. I can't believe it. After twenty-three years of marriage you're just going to throw it away? I can get you help."

"Help? Why do I need help?"

"For your addiction."

Louise snorted, a characteristic Mackenzie copied often when she was exasperated or annoyed. "I don't have an addiction, unless wanting to spend time with someone who is interested in me, how I feel, and makes me feel needed, wanted and cared about. If it's an addiction, it's not one I want to get rid of." She was infuriated, her words just jumbling out of her, whether or not she made any sense. It was all she could do to keep her voice low and not scream at him for being insane.

Louise pulled away. The dance was over as far as she was concerned, but he grabbed her arm and swung her back to him, holding tightly. He snarled at her, "You're mine. You've been mine for twenty-three years and I'm not giving you the divorce so you can lose yourself in some crazy, make-believe world."

She jerked her arm away. "We'll see about that!" Then she stormed off the dance floor.

Mackenzie frowned at her father as Louise strode off in a huff. She was about to follow her mother, albeit she wasn't sure if it would be better to let Louise have some time to cool down or not, when a presence behind her made himself known.

"Everything alright?" The man's voice startled Mackenzie.

Turning around, she couldn't help but realize he was one of Skye's groomsmen. Although no one could compare with Skye's classic Adonis good looks and gorgeous turquoise eyes, this one was more to her liking. Dark, rugged, handsome. With rich, brown hair and gray eyes, she couldn't help but notice him earlier and had to admit she'd been watching him throughout the day. During the reception her focus was on her mother and she'd lost track of this handsome man in lieu of familial issues. Now he was by her side and thoughts of her parents immediately evaporated. "Excuse me?"

"Sorry. I didn't mean to intrude. I just noticed you didn't appear happy at whatever is going on with that couple."

"Those are my parents." She licked her suddenly dry lips, her nerves frayed with him so close.

"Oh. I'm sorry." He ran a hand through his hair. "Family spats in public can be embarrassing, to say the least." He watched her for a minute. She was beautiful. Not overly slim, which was great with him. He liked women with a bit of meat on their bones. She had long brown hair, loosely braided into a fancy hairdo, with wisps haphazardly peeking out. Her eyes were a light-color hazel and he found them extremely striking. "I'm Caleb, by the way. A friend of Skye's."

"Since you're one of his groomsmen, I assumed as much." She smiled. "I'm Mackenzie. Daughter to the couple that seems intent on making scenes in public, as well as the woman who is Kendall's matron of honor."

He laughed, a rich, deep sound, and it sent warm fuzzies all the way down her body into her toes.

"How about if you dance with me and ignore the fact you're related to them? Then those who don't know better won't put you in the same category."

She hesitated, but only for a moment. "I appreciate the sentiment, but I think it's too late for people to not know I'm their daughter. However, that's been going on for years. Dancing with you, I

might not have another opportunity. I'd love to."
She took his outstretched hand as he led her onto
the dance floor, only giving one quick glance back
to where her mother disappeared.

Caleb glided her gracefully around the floor.
She'd admit she wasn't the greatest dancer, but he
maneuvered her around so expertly that she felt like
a pro and they should be trying out for *So You Think
You Can Dance*.

"How does your mother know Kendall?"

"She met Kendall in a store. They were both
grabbing at some clearance item and there was only
one left. The two of them started talking and once
Kendall mentioned her feline, Tinkerbell, Mom was
hooked. The two of them became fast friends as
they realized how much they had in common. And
what do you do for a living? Are you a dancer like
Skye?"

Caleb laughed again. "Shit no. I can manage to
do this slow stuff, and even a bit of the modern stuff
without making a complete fool of myself, but no
one needs to see me attempting to gyrate my junk in

a woman's face."

"He's not doing that anymore, is he?"

"No. When the club burned down, he'd already been planning on quitting. It was just something fun to do. After he met Kendall, though, he'd no desire to continue dancing for anyone but her."

"That's so romantic."

"I'll take your word on that. I know they had a rough start, but they seem to be doing great now."

"I heard about the events that put Kendall and Skye together. I'm glad he was there to save her life so many times."

"It was a bit scary for a while, that's for sure." He looked down into Mackenzie's eyes. "I understand he became interested in her the moment he saw her. Until now, I didn't think it was possible to be so attracted to someone immediately."

He grinned as he watched the blush spread across her cheeks. He'd hoped she felt the same way, and since she didn't seem to balk at the notion, he could only hope she did.

"Did you come because of your mother, or do

you know Kendall too?"

"I know her too. I met her through my mom, but we became friends as well. Not as close as she is with my mother, but I think she's just missing her own so much she sort of adopted mine. I don't mind, though. I never had a sister, or brother for that matter, so it's nice to have a bit more family. I know she's an only child as well, so we have that in common."

"And your dad?"

"Surprisingly, he's friends with Skye. They met on some golf course for a benefit a couple of years ago and just stayed in touch. Although, Dad doesn't golf as much as he used to. I'm not sure either realized the other would be here tonight."

"I'm glad you're here though."

"So am I," she stated softly, looking up at him. "I hope you don't mind my saying this, but I noticed you immediately when I entered the church. I'm glad you sought me out tonight."

He gripped her tighter about the waist. "I noticed you as well. I couldn't keep my eyes off of you."

"You never did answer me as to what you do, other than you aren't a dancer. Are you a fireman?"

Before he could answer, Louise was pulling the two of them apart. "Sorry to interrupt, but Mackenzie, you need to drive me home now!"

Makenzie threw Caleb an apologetic, embarrassed look. "Why? Didn't you drive here?"

"Yes, but your father slashed my tires and I refuse to stay here under his harassment, nor will I turn to him for assistance, as I know that's what he's hoping I'll do."

Caleb stepped forward. "Do you want to get the police involved? Can you prove he slashed the tires?"

"I don't know who you are, young man, but I saw him do it. So, yeah, I know he slashed them. He said this way he'd have to take me home, like I don't know about Uber or Lyft. I swear, Mackenzie, he's trying to keep me in the Stone Age or something. Barefoot and in the kitchen. I'm too old for the pregnant part, but I'm not his slave. Will you drive me home or am I calling for a ride?"

"Yes. I'll drive you home. What about your car?"

"It can stay here the night. I'll deal with a tow and tires on Monday morning when it's not as expensive due to the weekend." Louise turned and headed back to the door without another word.

"I'm sorry. Thanks for the dance." Mackenzie raced to catch up with her mother, leaving Caleb standing on the edge of the dance floor. He hadn't even gotten Mackenzie's phone number.

He could only hope she'd return to the reception once she dropped her mother off at home, then realized he didn't even know Mackenzie's last name or where they lived. He rushed out in hopes of finding her, but they were already gone by the time he reached the parking lot.

Chapter Two

One week before the murder:

Tyler Channing looked around the hotel lobby. His wife checked in an hour ago and sent him a text with the room number so he could just escape to the room without hanging around the lobby. Although he was in the public eye, he liked his privacy and had to gear himself up mentally in order to face crowds of fans. He was grateful when the elevator doors slid open and the car was empty. At the last moment before the doors fully shut, a hand slipped between them, forcing them to open once again. A middle-aged woman with brown hair pulled back in a ponytail slipped inside, giving him a smile and, looking at the pushed floor button, she stepped back.

"Welcome to Valley View, Tyler. Did you have a nice trip?"

He was slightly taken aback from her forwardness. "Um. Fine, thank you."

She gave him a piercing look. "You don't

remember me, do you."

He turned to her and looked her over more closely. She was about 5'6" and a bit overweight, but still attractive. Her brown hair was peppered with streaks of gray, and the crow's feet around her dark brown eyes made her look older than he was sure she was. Although she looked slightly familiar, he couldn't place it and figured she just reminded him of a thousand others he'd met over his lifetime. The elevator doors opened and they both stepped out. He turned to face her. "Sorry. No, I don't."

"It's okay. It's been quite a few years. Louise. Back then I was Louise Madden, now it's Harper."

He grimaced at not recalling who she was or where he'd met her previously. "I'm sorry."

Disappointed, she gave him a single nod. "Don't worry about it. We can catch up later."

Before he could respond, she turned and walked down the hallway. He stood stunned for a moment, still trying to remember meeting a woman named Louise. Giving his head a slight shake, he headed towards his room and forgot about her. He had more important things to think about.

He knocked on the penthouse suite door, knowing there'd be a key waiting for him inside. As Debra opened the door, he pulled her into a tight embrace. His twenty-year-old daughter, Pearl, glanced up from the television and nodded a greeting while his personal assistant, Maggie Keeler, stood to greet him with her notebook fanned out. She stood aside patiently as she waited for him to acknowledge her after he kissed his wife.

"Hey, Maggie. So, what's on my schedule for today?" He gave Debra a slap on her rump as he moved to the dining table next to Maggie.

"You have an appointment with the director at 3:00 at the theater. I'll have a car waiting for you at 2:45. Then dinner with the mayor and his family at 5:30 at the Blue Ox Steak House. The car will wait for you to take you from the theater to the restaurant. I've got another car picking up Debra and Pearl to meet you there."

Tyler nodded, glancing at his watch. It was only 10:30, so he had a few hours to relax and go over his script and the notes he wished to discuss with the director.

A knock on the door sent Maggie scurrying to open it. A bellman stood there with a basket of gummies in various shapes and sizes. She gave the bellman a tip, accepting the basket and bringing it over to the dining table. Pulling out the card, she handed it to Tyler.

Tyler loved gummy candy. It was one of his true downfalls, but not something most people knew. Someone certainly did their homework and he was curious to know who was so thoughtful to send such a fabulous treat. He suspected it was the theater company, or even the director welcoming him to Valley View.

Debra moved up beside him, noting his frown as he read the card. "Who's it from?"

He waved the card and then tossed it back into the basket. "Some woman named Louise Harper."

"Do you know her?"

"Not exactly." He wasn't sure how to explain.

Debra crossed her arms, her brows furrowing.

"What exactly does that mean?"

And there it was, that touch of jealously coursing through Debra's veins. True, Tyler had been caught in some compromising positions in the past, but he'd been faithful recently. Still, he couldn't blame her for being suspicious. He doubted she'd ever fully trust him again. "It's from this woman named Louise; I just met her in the elevator. Although she says we've met before a long time ago, I just don't remember her."

Debra looked at the basket, overflowing with her husband's favorite treats. "One of your conquests?"

Tyler sighed, running a hand through his thick head of blond hair. "Look. I know you don't trust me, and I can't blame you, but I've been faithful since you caught me with Sherry and gave me the ultimatum. I chose you. I don't regret that. However, that being said, I don't remember her and I usually remember the names of those women I had relations with. I have no recognition of Louise, and having seen her in the elevator, even less so. Could be someone I worked with years ago and I just don't remember."

Debra hesitated for several minutes, then relaxed her stance. "Okay. Sorry."

As she started to move past him, he grabbed her hand and pulled her close, his arms encircling her waist. "I love you. No one else but you. I'm sorry I ever did anything to make you doubt my sincerity. Hell, she might even have something to do with this production and this was her way of welcoming me to the theater. I'll probably see her at the director's meeting later today when I meet the rest of the cast and production crew. As for having met her before, who knows when or where?" He could feel his little speech softened her even more as she relaxed in his embrace. He leaned over to take her lips with his.

Pearl looked over at them from the couch. She'd seen them go through some rough times and it thrilled her to no end that they were getting along so well. After all, what child wants to see their parents be split apart? She'd known of her father's affairs before her mother did, and it killed her to know they were having those kinds of marital problems. She thought she was destined to be one of the many Hollywood children who came from a divided home. Pearl couldn't be happier she'd been proven wrong.

Standing, she flipped off the television and nodded to Maggie. "I'm going to go explore. Maggie, would you like to join me? I'd love your input since you were raised here."

Maggie realized Pearl was arranging for her parents to have some private time and quickly agreed. "I'd love to show you around." Turning slightly, she lowered her eyes as she spoke to Tyler. "I'll be back in plenty of time to assist you getting prepared for the theater."

The women didn't wait for an answer as they quickly departed the hotel room, leaving Debra and Tyler alone.

Chapter Three

Tyler entered the back of the theater and let his eyes adjust to the dim interior. He had a sense of déjà vu, but he wasn't certain if it was because most theaters were very similar and he'd been in enough of them to call them home, or if it were something else altogether. Threading his way past the dressing rooms and backdrops being worked on, he found his way to the director's office and knocked on the frosted-glass door, etched with the words Byron Cassiday.

"Come in," a deep, rough voice indicating years of smoking called to him.

Entering, Tyler looked around, that strong sense of having been there before overcoming him once again.

The older man, with gray hair; tanned, wrinkled, facial features; and a smoke-stained mustache, stood holding his hand out in greeting.

"Mr. Channing. I'm so glad you came. Have you had a chance to look over the script?"

"Thanks, and yes I did. I made a few notes I'd like to go over with you, if that's okay."

"If they are comments on the script itself, I'd rather you talk to the author, Kendall Roberts—I mean, Falcon. She just got married a couple of days ago and is currently on her honeymoon, but she'll be back in a few more days. Please, have a seat." He waved to the chair in front of his desk, sitting back down and pulling out a cigarette. "Can't seem to stop no matter how hard I try. Do you smoke?"

"No. I used to when I was younger. Some of the parts I had required me to do so, but I eventually quit and refuse to pick it up again, even for a role."

"Ah. I see what some of the things you wished to talk about are. I'm sure Mrs. Falcon won't have any issue changing the smoking scenes."

"That was only one of my concerns. I have a few others I'd like to discuss."

"Sure. We can talk about anything you like. Your P.A. already informed us of the particular things to have in your room each day: the type of water you prefer and your food preferences."

"Maggie is very efficient. I've no doubt she made you aware of several of my personal choices."

"She's from somewhere around here, I think."

"Yeah. She grew up in Valley View."

"Is that when you met her?"

"Excuse me?"

"Maggie. Did you meet her when you were in town before?"

"I don't believe I've ever been to Valley View in the past."

"Oh. I could've sworn you'd been here at the start of your career for a play called *The Hoosier Schoolmaster*."

"*The Hoosier Schoolmaster*?" Tyler's brow creased as he concentrated on the name, then his eyebrows lifted as realization dawned on him. "Shit. I totally forgot about that. The play never actually went on. We got as far as rehearsals, but the production had some serious issues and they shut it down before opening night due to lack of financing."

"Yeah. The previous managers embezzled the

funds a month prior and, though the director tried to keep the show going long enough to get the cash from ticket sales, he just couldn't do it."

Tyler rubbed his forehead in consternation. He'd put the whole experience out of his mind, quickly moving on to bigger and better productions immediately after. "I didn't meet Maggie while I was here for that show. I only found her a couple of years ago, as a recommendation from a colleague of mine. I'm not entirely sure how he met her, but he'd used her services for a couple of years and, when he no longer needed her, he suggested me hiring her. He knew I was looking for someone at the time and he was also aware of how much I appreciated efficiency. If nothing else, Maggie is extremely efficient."

"I noticed that was the case when she came to make sure everything was in order prior to your arrival."

The reminder of *The Hoosier Schoolmaster* resulted in a deeper introspection of trying to remember Louise. Maybe? Admittedly, the play was so boring he'd spent most of his time high just to pass the hours. Hell, he could've had sex with her and never remembered.

After their discussion, Byron led him around, showing Tyler the theater facilities and introducing him to some of the other cast members. During the tour, Tyler was sure they were being watched. When he thought he saw someone out of the corner of his eye or a shadow cross his path, they were suddenly gone. He wished he knew for sure if it was just an overactive imagination, but Byron didn't appear to notice anything amiss. It could just be glimpses of the backstage crew moving about, but he couldn't find anyone doing so. He was used to the workings of a theater, yet he couldn't seem to get past the eerie feeling coursing over him.

He had to admit he was grateful when Byron showed him his private dressing room. A moment of peace before he headed out to dinner was much appreciated. Plopping on the couch, one leg dangling over the side, one arm draped over his eyes, he let out a soft sigh of emotional exhaustion.

It didn't last long, however. It was only a moment later when he heard a slight rustling sound and knew he was no longer alone in the room. Did Byron forget something?

But it wasn't Byron that was sitting across from him when he moved his arm away from his eyes. Standing quickly, surprise evident on Tyler's face, he knew instantly that this woman from the elevator was who he'd been sensing on his tour around the building.

"Louise? Right?"

She grinned with pride that he recognized her and bobbed her head rapidly. "Yes. I was hoping you'd remember."

"Actually, I only recall you from the elevator. I assume we met the last time I was in town all those years ago, but truthfully, I don't remember much at all of that time. I barely recall being in this town, and I only do so thanks to Byron jogging my memory slightly. I'm very sorry I don't recollect more."

Louise stood and moved in front of him. Her

hands glided softly over his chest as she batted her brown eyes at him. "It's okay. I know you'll remember everything about us, given time."

Tyler frowned. He hated to upset a fan, but she was being way too forward with him. Maybe it was his fault. Maybe he was more intimate with her the last time he was in town and now she expected it to be the same way. He grabbed her wrists and held them tightly away from his body. "Sorry. I don't play around. I'm a happily married man."

Surprised, Louise didn't pull away from him. "I don't believe that. At least not that you're happy. But I'll play your game. For the moment." She added the last bit as she pulled out of his firm grip.

He grit his teeth, his jaw working as he tried to contemplate a way to further discourage her. "It's not a game. I'm not interested. Please leave my dressing room." It took every ounce of control to not cuss her out or push her through the door and slam it in her face, but his patience was wearing thin and he couldn't promise his control would last indefinitely.

Louise stepped away. "I'll leave. But know I'll not be far away. We're meant to be together, even if you can't see it just yet." She gave him a knowing smirk before she slipped out the door.

Only when the door closed behind her did he let out a sigh of relief. God forbid his wife found out about Louise being in his dressing room or following him about. He had the feeling he probably had been intimate with Louise way back when. However, it was his first real acting job, his first time at having any real money for what he loved doing and he was young. What better way than to get lost to alcohol and drugs since he had the money to afford it. Yeah, he was high almost from the time he came to the town and got the official script to the time the play closed. He couldn't get out of Valley View fast enough, and thankfully his agent already had another role for him, but only if he cleaned up to audition for it. A television role on a sitcom, a dream part. It was while doing that show he met Debra. Sober and drug free, though it had been hard to clean up in the months succeeding

Valley View, he landed the role of a lifetime and really launched his career, never looking back.

He'd almost lost Debra a few years back when he started to fool around behind her back. And when she'd caught him cheating, he was sure she was going to file for divorce. Instead, Debra wanted to try couple's counseling, and today they were back together and stronger than ever before. He wasn't about to screw it up again. Not that he'd any inclination to do so with Louise, who so wasn't his type. But he didn't need the woman causing problems in his marriage, either. Debra was already suspicious because of the basket of gummies Louise sent to him. Damn, he'd almost forgotten about those. In any other circumstance he'd have thanked her for such a treat, but now it was just too awkward. He'd have to send a note to Maggie to have her get rid of them before he got back to the room. It didn't feel right to eat them after this current confrontation, even if they were given to him as a welcome gift. Somehow, it just seemed like she was expecting some sort of a return on them, and he didn't like the price she was going to ask.

Looking around the room, he gave a decisive nod. Time to move past Louise and her antics. He was sure he set her straight, now, and she'd leave him alone. Glancing at the small clock on the dresser, he realized it was time to meet the limo for dinner with the mayor.

Chapter Four

Mayor John Davis tilted his head back, letting out a loud, boisterous laugh, startling those around his table. His poised wife blushed delicately, dropping her eyes at the attention her husband drew. Mary was not one to be in the public's eye as much as her husband was. She preferred to remain behind the scenes, dealing with raising their two children: twelve-year-old Alice and ten-year-old Simon. The latter two could barely sit still through the meal at the Blue Ox, jumping up to chase the dessert cart or use the restroom at least a dozen times throughout the course of their meal, finding the whole affair dull.

Tyler was so grateful Pearl had long ago outgrown that youthful restlessness. He reached over and squeezed Debra's hand, bringing it to his lips in order to keep from snapping at the lack of control the mayor seemed to have over his family. If he couldn't control them, how was he able to handle the whole town?

The waiter brought over brandy sniffers for the adults and a couple of kiddie cocktails for the Davis children.

John picked up his glass, swirling the amber liquid around slightly. "I know toasts should be made over something like wine, but this brandy is a local treat, made right down by the old mill we have near Lake Emily. Old Mill Brandies make theirs from various fruits, depending on the season. Strawberries are the current flavor base, and one of my personal favorites. They do fruit wines as well, but I'm partial to the brandies. Have you had them before?"

Tyler shook his head as he reached for his own sniffer. "No. I don't think so. I'm not a brandy drinker by trade, but I admit I'm curious over the local prospects." He couldn't help but notice the dark look his wife gave him. Having given up all drugs and most alcohol, except for the special occasion, he understood her concerns, but he was past the get-drunk stage and a couple of swallows wouldn't hurt. He gave her a wink to reassure her, then tilted the rim of the glass his to lips. The sweetness burned the back of his throat as it slid down into his belly, warming up everything in its amber path. "Wow. That's..." He wasn't sure how to describe it.

"I know, right? It's delicious. We are very proud of our brandy production." John grinned.

"Yes. You should be proud. It's delicious." Tyler set the glass down, grateful he was a decent enough actor to get him past how awful he thought the concoction was. The liquor was way too sweet for his personal liking. He couldn't fool Debra, though, as she used the napkin to dab her lips in order to hide her small chuckle.

Grabbing her hand, Tyler gave it a tight squeeze so she wouldn't blow his cover as he smiled at the mayor. His smile, however, quickly faded when he felt a hand on his shoulder.

"Mayor Davis. How good to see you and Mary. The kids are looking bigger each time I see them."

John looked up and grinned. "Louise. Have you met Mr. Channing and his wife, Debra, or his daughter, Pearl?"

Tyler swore all the blood left his cheeks as he stared at Louise. He couldn't believe she was there, and now he was worried she'd cause trouble for him.

"I've not met Debra or Pearl. I met Tyler years ago and again earlier today." Louise moved to the other side of Tyler, her hand never leaving his shoulders.

Debra didn't miss the fact of Louise being so familiar with her husband. "Louise? I think my *husband* mentioned your name today. You were the one who sent the basket of gummies, were you not?" She was going to make it painfully clear Louise was not going to get away with anything, especially when it came to her husband. "Those are one of the only treats he can't resist."

Debra's veiled meaning wasn't lost on Louise. "Yes. I was. I know his tastes well," Louise countered. After seeing Tyler's wife in person, she couldn't help but wonder why he was so hung up on her. She was the total opposite of Louise: blonde, thin, with a polished air of snobbery. She couldn't imagine Tyler with anyone so superficial. She wondered how much plastic surgery Tyler bought for her to appear so artificial. Their daughter, Pearl, seemed just like her mother, with a mini-me attitude.

Debra's eyes darkened. "Oh? Funny, because he certainly doesn't remember yours."

Those words touched a raw nerve in Louise, who picked up the glass of brandy and threw it in Debra's face, giggling as the woman screeched and stood, the amber liquid streaming down her hair and checks onto her once-pristine golden dress.

Tyler jumped to his feet and pulled Louise back. "How dare you? Who do you think you are? I don't know you, or if I ever did, I don't remember you. Stay away from me and my family. Or I'll make you wish you did. Got it?" He grabbed his wife's arm. "Mayor, thank you for dinner, but I'm afraid we are done for the evening."

While he was talking to Louise and John, Mary handed Debra her napkin to help her wipe her face as best as she could. Tyler didn't wait for her to freshen up more as he jerked her out of the restaurant, calling for Pearl to come as well.

Pearl hesitated, wondering who Louise was or what all the fuss was about, even though she had a slight inkling. Surely her father wasn't interested in this overly obnoxious woman.

Louise followed them. "You think we don't have something between us? You might pretend to not remember, but I've got the proof that we were just together the other night," she snarled. "He's mine. He's always been mine," she shrieked.

Tyler stopped and swung around, seemingly unaware that he was dragging Debra with him as he turned. "Listen, bitch. I wasn't with you or anyone else the other night. Whatever your so-called proof is is nothing but malicious fabrications, and neither I nor my family will be a party to it. This is your last warning. If you don't stay away from us, I'll be forced to apply for an Order of Protection against you."

As Tyler swung about, four policemen entered

the establishment, immediately assessing the situation. "What's going on? We got a complaint you were harassing a woman?" They approached Tyler, who was holding tightly to Debra's upper arm, still dripping wet from the drink Louise threw on her.

"No," Debra spoke up. "This is my husband. That woman," she pointed to Louise, "has been harassing us and threw a drink on me."

While Debra gave her statement to one officer, two others took statements from the mayor and his family as well as a few onlookers seated around them. The final officer talked to Louise. Several minutes later, they had Louise in handcuffs, leading her to a squad car. Louise thrashed about, kicking at one of the officers as he tried to put her in the back of the squad car.

"Let me go! I didn't do anything!" she screamed as she fought.

It took two men to get her under control enough to stick her in the vehicle. "Settle down now or you'll be in more trouble than you already are."

"Do you need us to sign a complaint?" Debra gloated over Louise's arrest.

"You can just show up at her court date to make it official," Officer Simon stated. "Mr. Channing, on behalf of Valley View, we're sorry your arrival to our town has been hampered by such ugliness. Ma'am, please enjoy the rest of your stay in Valley View."

"Thank you, officer. Are we free to go? I'm getting intoxicated by just breathing the fumes from my outfit and hair."

"Yes, ma'am. You're free to go. We have your information if we need anything else."

Tyler didn't waste any time leading his family outside to the waiting car service. Pearl and Debra were quiet the whole ride back to the hotel, and every time Tyler started to speak, Debra threw him a dark look, which caused him to immediately quiet down. He knew she was furious at him, and it annoyed him because she was so angry when he did nothing to deserve it.

The ride seemed to last forever even though the

hotel was only ten minutes from the restaurant. The air in the vehicle was so tense, one could cut it with a knife. Once they arrived, Debra and Pearl were out of the car almost before the vehicle made a full stop. Pearl dashed into the building without a second glance, but Debra leaned back in and snarled at her husband. "I suggest you don't come in for a while. I think we all need space at the moment." She slammed the car door as she proceeded to head inside the building.

Tyler hopped out and rushed to grab her arm, pulling her around to press against his hard chest, holding her immobile against him. "I didn't do anything. And if I did, with her, it was eons ago. I've told her I'm not interested in her. I've told her I'm married. I know you don't trust me, but trust me on this. Does she even look like my type? Why are you angry at me when I've done nothing wrong this time? Get over yourself. You want to hate her, be my guest and join the club. I detest what she's doing to me, to us, but don't let her win by pushing me away."

Debra stopped struggling. She could feel the eyes of the onlookers stopping to watch them and her cheeks flamed red. "Fine. We can finish discussing this inside." She tried to push him away, but she was so small compared to him her efforts proved useless.

He cocked a lopsided smile as he leaned down to kiss her softly, feeling her melt, albeit slightly unwillingly, against him. Stepping back, he slid his hands down her arm, taking her hand to lead her inside. "I'd hoped we were done discussing it and could go right to the you-make-it-up-to-me sex."

Chapter Five

Six days before the murder:

"What the hell did you think you were doing?" Al snarled at Louise, not caring she was being led out of the holding cell by a police officer. He stood with his legs slightly apart, his beefy arms folded over his chest.

Louise didn't answer him, but looked past him to their daughter. "Why did you call him?"

"Sorry, Mom. It's not like I have $1,000 just lying around to bail you out of jail."

"I'd've rather sat in jail than have to be indebted to him."

"In case you haven't noticed, I'm standing right here." Al signed some release papers for Louise, then followed the two women out of the Valley View Police Station. Hurrying to catch up, he thrust the papers at Louise. "Your court date is in one month and you can't bother Mr. Channing or his family again."

"I wasn't bothering Mr. Channing. And his

family started it."

"Mom! From what I heard, Mr. Channing feels you're stalking him. That's just creepy."

Louise stopped and gazed at them both. "Look. I get you're not too happy with me now. It's that woman who forced the issue. And Tyler is the kind of guy who won't embarrass others in public. I appreciate you bailed me out of jail, but I've got a relationship with Tyler and I'm not going to stay away."

"First off, that woman is his wife. Second, I'm still your husband, at least until I sign those divorce papers you had me served with, so I'm telling you to stay away from all of them. I won't bail you out again. And third, you just met the guy, how can you possibly have a relationship with him?"

"Wait. Mom, you don't think that stupid game you play on Facebook is really him, do you? Just 'cause you play with someone who uses his profile picture.

Al stopped, his eyebrow raised in questioning surprise. "What are you talking about Mac?"

Mackenzie turned to her father. "That role-play stuff she spends on her computer all the time. The guy she plays with uses Tyler Channing's pictures as his character's appearance."

"No. No. That's not it at all. You don't understand. Neither of you understand."

"Then explain it to us." Al folded his arms across his chest once again.

Louise rubbed her forehead. "Look, it's late and I'm tired. Can we all just discuss this another time?" She started to move past each of them, but Al quickly blocked her path once again.

"No. We can't discuss it another time. Not if you're going to keep harassing the Channing family. I want to know what the fuck this is all about. What is your obsession with this man?"

"I don't owe you any explanation. I didn't ask for you to bail me out, and I didn't ask for you to come here. I'm not your wife anymore, despite the fact you haven't signed the divorce papers yet. I'm getting the divorce, one way or another, and I don't want you a part of my life. As such, you've no business in what I do or don't do."

"I can't believe you feel that way, Mom. I called him to help because you called me. Are you going to say I'm no longer your daughter either? I want to know what's going on too. It's not just Dad."

Louise peered at the young woman. She couldn't deny the woman was her daughter. Louise had looked pretty much the same at her age, despite not having aged as gracefully as she would've liked. Louise dyed her hair to hide most of the grays that otherwise crept in, but they still came back first near the temples. She had far too many wrinkles from sun exposure and a hard life. Mackenzie had none of that yet, and Louise hoped Mackenzie would fare better as she aged.

Louise wanted to tell Mackenzie everything, but she was frightened to do so. It was a secret she'd had for ages and not something she was willing to admit. Remaining quiet was easier, yet she knew no one was going to move unless she gave some sort of explanation. "Yes, he is the avatar for the person who I play with on Facebook. But he is also that person."

"What? That doesn't make any sense."

"Are you even listening to yourself? Louise, you're nuts if you think he's part of your game. He has a life and much better things to do than to sit at a computer all day playing some idiotic fantasy endeavor that you find entertaining."

"See. I knew neither of you'd understand. I know it seems like I'm mental or something, but I know Tyler and I know that's him I'm on the computer with. He just can't admit it because he's so famous. So he pretends he's someone else using Tyler's pictures, even though I know otherwise. I know you don't believe me, but I'm not wrong."

"You're right. We don't believe you. It's just not possible. Someone that good looking and busy with his family and work could in no way spend as much time on the stupid computer as you do. You've made it your life, Louise. You focus on nothing other than that game and you're losing sight of the real world. You're absolutely nuts if you think he's the one sitting at the other end of the computer playing with you. Can't you see that? He has no idea who you are, and I doubt if he cares to find out."

"You don't know anything, Al. You're so buried with your work; how would you know what I do or don't do. And Mackenzie moved out a couple of years ago. I sit at home, alone, and that person at the other end of the computer is my best friend. I know it seems strange, but I've gotten to know him well. I talk to him daily, and not just about the game. We talk. I know he's married, but he's not happy in his marriage and suffers through it because it's easier than separating or getting a divorce. I know he works, and he likes his job and can't really talk to me when he is working. I know he's on vacation this week with his family. It's not a coincidence that this is the week he got here and is settling in for Kendall's new play at the theater. Don't you get it? It's Tyler. It's been Tyler all along, and now he's here, in town, with me. I know neither of you get it. I know neither of you will ever understand that Tyler gives me something I need. He makes me feel alive and wanted. Desired, even. Something I hadn't felt in years. Believe what you want or don't want. I don't care. I know the truth, even if you can't see it."

Louise moved past them, hailing a cab. She left them both standing on the curb, their mouths agape at her little speech. When the taxi drove out of sight, Al scratched the back of his head. "Mackenzie, I don't know what to do."

"I know, Dad. I kinda feel the same way. I think mentally she's slipping slightly. Confusing real life with that fantasy one. I just don't know what to do to help her."

"I'm not sure anything can be done. I'll tell you this, though: she may have filed for divorce, but I don't have to sign the papers. There will come a time when she realizes it's not actually Tyler and she's going to need us both."

Mackenzie sighed. "I don't know how she's going to handle it if you don't give her the divorce. Thanks for coming, though, and bailing her out of jail. I couldn't handle it if she had to stay in there for any extended period of time. She needs help, but jail isn't going to give it to her."

"Yeah, she does, but I'm not sure she's ready to accept any help just yet. And if she's not ready to accept it, there's no reason to give it to her. She has to be willing to realize the truth and deal with it. Until then, there's nothing we can do. She'll only rebel more until she's ready."

"I know. Doesn't mean I gotta like it. Thankfully, we still have our weekly going to church followed by brunch each Sunday. I'll keep working on her and hopefully she'll wake up and smell the coffee." Mackenzie gave her dad a hug. "I'd best be getting home. Charlie needs to be walked." Charlie being her Alaskan Husky.

"Glad I could help. Love you, Mac."

Chapter Six

After picking up her car from the restaurant, where it was left when she was arrested, Louise headed to the hotel. She knew, deep inside, she should go home, but she had to see him. Even if it was from only a distance. She knew what room he was in, from earlier in the day, and which street the windows overlooked. She had her binoculars with her, which she pulled out once she was parked. The draperies were mostly closed, but there was a slight crack in the bedroom one. Nothing she could pierce, though. However, the living area was still wide open. Would she be lucky? She hoped so.

She wasn't sure how long she was there staring at that window, the binoculars in her lap, but after a long while, her heart beat faster and her breath hitched when Tyler stood by the window peering out, a glass of wine in his hand. Her mouth ran dry. God, he was a good-looking man with broad shoulders and a narrow waist. His arms were thick, not flabby like Al's, and of pure muscle. His short blond hair had that slight wave in the front. And though she couldn't see them, his piercing hazel eyes always sent shivers down her spine. When she was in his presence earlier that day, the looks he gave her sent chills racing to her toes. She could only imagine what it would be like to kiss him.

Lifting the binoculars, she could see he was talking to someone out of her line of sight. She wondered what he was saying in that deep, rich voice he had. She couldn't help herself. Holding the binoculars with one hand, she used the other to rub herself, imagining it was his hand and not her own. In her mind, she replayed some of the words he wrote as part of their Facebook play. She was lost in the fantasy her mind created. Putting the binoculars aside, she closed her eyes, peeking open every few moments to check and see if he was still by the window. When she was ready to finish up, he'd moved away, so she closed her eyes and let herself give a release to her pent-up desire.

Panting softly, she opened her eyes again just in time to see him come to the window and close the drapes. How symbolic. It was as if he chose that exact moment to say goodnight to her. She sat there a few more minutes before she started up the car and finally headed home.

Once inside her own abode, Louise double-locked the door behind her. She'd take a shower in a few minutes and get ready for bed, but she needed to do a couple of things first. At the top of that list was turning on the computer to see if he'd been on at all. Not surprising, he hadn't. She'd hoped he would've said something about their meeting today or about his bitch having her arrested. However, *Debra* was probably keeping close tabs on him after their encounter in the restaurant. God, how she detested that woman—so snide and pretentious. No wonder Tyler wasn't happy in his marriage.

Then she went to the attic for her hope chest, which she'd kept locked for the past twenty-three years. Inside were pictures of a much younger Tyler while he'd been in Valley View at the Pixard Theater. Al and Mackenzie may have thought she was mentally unstable, but she had proof they were together all those years ago. Although why he kept saying he didn't remember her, when he clearly did, baffled her. Maybe it was another game: one to appease his own wife and daughter. She looked through some additional papers within the chest, then took all of the pictures and papers to her desk downstairs.

The truth would come out soon enough, and when it did she'd have the paper trail to back it up. Then they'd all know she wasn't screwed up in the head. They'd realize she'd been telling them part of the truth all along. They'd understand she couldn't tell anyone everything before, but things were different now. Things *would* be different now. And she'd make sure of it. She'd get rid of *Debra* for him. She had the nerve to do what must be done, and when his wife was gone, Louise knew he'd turn to her, openly. He'd be able to go to her in front of the whole world then. And everything would be perfect. Just as she dreamed it would be. Just as they'd talked about on Facebook and in chat. The thought of them finally being together made her blood run hot and she stripped off her clothes as she headed to take a pulsating shower to cool off her desires.

Chapter Seven

Five days before the murder:

Mackenzie pulled up to the house and got out, clicking the key fob to lock her car doors. It was early and she was sure her mom would still be asleep, or at best just making coffee. Mac wanted a few minutes alone in the morning light to reason with her mother calmly over the whole Tyler Channing business. Over the past few years she'd noticed her mother occasionally losing grip on her reality. There were times when her mother seemed to think some television show she had watched was reality. Granted, there were enough so-called reality television shows to confuse anyone, but some of them, such as *The Rookie* or *The Good Doctor*, were not reality based. And since Louise started playing on the computer, those instances seemed to come more frequently. Now Mackenzie was sure her mother had lost her sanity, unable to tell the difference between reality and fiction, confusing her role-play with actuality. As far as Mac was concerned, her mother needed help.

She retrieved the spare key and let herself in, calling out as she did so. "Mom? It's Mackenzie. Are you still sleeping?"

"No." Louise peeked out from the kitchen, a smile on her face. "What a great surprise. I was just making coffee. Can I make you some breakfast? Are you able to stay for a bit?"

Mackenzie moved towards her mom, giving her a hug. "Yeah. I don't have to be at work until ten." She followed her mom into the kitchen, sitting down at the kitchen table.

Louise grabbed a mug from her cabinet and poured a cup of the hot black liquid into it before bringing it over to Mackenzie. The sugar and cream were already on the table.

"Why do I feel this isn't totally a social call?" Louise headed back to the stove where she had a couple of eggs waiting to be put into the pan.

"Probably because it isn't. Mom, I love you. I'd do anything for you. But I'm worried about you and this obsession you've got with Tyler Channing. It's not healthy and it's not natural."

"How do you even know it's an obsession? He only arrived in town two days ago."

"And in one day you have bothered him so much he's had you arrested."

"No. *He* didn't. That woman, Debra did."

"You mean his wife? I don't blame her. If you were bothering my husband, if I had a husband, I'd have you arrested too. He's married and seems to be happily so. He's not the guy you play with on your computer. That guy, if he's even a guy, only *uses* pictures of Tyler. It's not actually him."

"Normally, I'd agree with you, Mac." She flipped the eggs, concentrating so as not to burn them. "But you don't have all the facts. The person I play with online knows things that happened years ago that only Tyler would know. We play, yes, and that's make-believe. But we also talk in chat and that's real life."

"Anything that person would know about you is something you told them when you first started talking. Tyler is way too busy to play a silly game, and least of all with—"

"With a nobody like me?" Louise let the eggs slip out of the pan and onto a plate before cracking a couple more into the pan. She brought the plate and utensils over to Mackenzie, setting the steaming eggs in front of her.

"That's not what I meant. He's a famous person, with a family. I don't know of anyone famous person who role-plays on the computer. It's unheard of."

"Because they want to remain anonymous. It's a chance to just be normal without having such expectations of their fans watching their every move, or the paparazzi waiting to get the dirty scoop on them and sell it to the highest bidder for the tabloids. It's a chance to be ordinary and not totally in the public's eye."

Mackenzie pulled the coffee closer to her, holding it within her hands and enjoying the warmth. Although it was 78 degrees, she was still a bit chilled. "I admit that's a reasonable assumption, but Tyler isn't one of those actors hiding their true identity on a Facebook game."

"How can you be so certain?"

"Because, Mom. It just is."

Louise snorted softly into her coffee cup. "Is that anything like, 'Because I say so?'" She took a hesitant sip of the dark, hot liquid. "Look, I understand you find it hard to believe, but it's all true. And the thing is, there's more that I never told you or Al. Or anyone for that matter." Setting the cup down, she kept it between her hands. "There isn't any easy way to say this. I've been waiting for the right time to tell you, but it just never seemed to be the right time. However, you need to know the truth. Tyler is your biological father."

Mackenzie had been taking a sip of her coffee when the shock of the news hit her like a ton of bricks, causing her to spew the coffee from her mouth in a fine spray across the table and onto her mother's arms. She sat stunned, but only for a moment. Her shocked disbelief quickly turned to anger, and she stood quickly, not caring that she spilled the rest of the coffee in her cup or that the liquid went onto the plate of eggs her mother had prepared for her.

"How dare you? Have you lost your mind? It's impossible!"

"No, it's not. Tyler was here in Valley View before for a play. His career was just starting and I had a small bit part, but we got closer and you were the result of our interlude."

"Why are you so consumed with…? I don't even know what to call it…obsession? With this guy that you're now making things up, like my parenthood? I can't believe you'd say something so underhanded. You're sick, Mom. I love you, but you've lost your mind and seriously need help. I see now, I'm not qualified to help you, so I'm telling you to get professional help!" Mackenzie scooped up her phone and purse, storming out of the kitchen. Her heart was racing with anger. She couldn't drive, not in the mental shape she was in. Her hands shook, her breathing heavy. Unlocking her phone, she dialed her dad, tapping her free hand on her bouncing knee as she waited for him to pick up.

"Come on. Come on, already. Answer the phone."

"Hello?" The rough, slightly hoarse voice greeted Mackenzie and she knew she had woke him up.

"Sorry, Dad. Didn't mean to disturb you so early. Can I come over? I need to talk to you about Mom."

Al could hear how upset she was, even over the phone, and with her mother being involved he could only imagine what had happened to put her in such an overwrought state. "Sure, Mac. You know you're always welcome. I'll put on a pot of coffee. The door'll be open. Just come on in, but drive safely. Whatever is going on isn't worth putting your life at risk by driving recklessly."

Just knowing he was a calm voice of reason, she took a deep breath. "I'll be careful. Thank you." She sniffled, and once she hung up the phone she reached for a tissue. She couldn't believe her mother would be so cruel as to make up such a ridiculous lie. Al had been a great father to her as she grew up, and to even suggest he wasn't her dad sent her into a tailspin. She dabbed her eyes, blew her nose and started the car, taking a deep breath. She needed to keep her promise and focus on her driving. True, he only lived a couple of miles away, but even this early in the morning, traffic in Valley View could be hazardous.

When Mackenzie arrived, she burst in the door and searched for her dad. No words, there would be time for all of that later. Right now, she needed her dad. As Al turned when she entered the room, he was taken aback at her almost tackling him, holding on for dear life. He wrapped his beefy arms around her, rubbing her back. Such a simple action broke every restraint she had been utilizing to keep in check. She broke down in heart-wrenching sobs.

"It's okay, Mac. Whatever it is, it'll be okay." Al rarely saw Mackenzie in such a distressingly emotional state.

"She's horrible. She's so horrible," Mac managed to get out through her lamenting.

Al grit his teeth, his jaw clenching tightly over whatever it was that Louise did or said to put Mac in such a state. Slowly, he managed to shift her over slightly so he could grab a box of tissue he kept on the counter. Handing her the whole box, he slowly guided her towards a chair so they could sit down, not once letting go of her. He waited until she was ready to tell him what was going on, his mind running away to all sorts of scenarios, especially since bailing Louise out of jail the previous evening. He wanted to know, but he held his tongue. Still, he couldn't help but reflect on how different Louise had been over the past couple of years. Ever since he bought her that computer for Christmas. Had he known how addictive she would've found it—or the disruption to their marriage, or even this obsession she seemed to have with Facebook—he'd never have gotten her one. Maybe if he hadn't, their marriage, their *life* wouldn't be quite so screwed up. Louise was his wife, and a part of him would always want her, but he couldn't deal with her on an everyday basis. He knew, given time, she'd come around and come back to him. Although he'd have to overlook a lot of her recent faults, she was his and she always would be. There was no way in hell he was going to sign those divorce papers.

"I know she can be horrible. What did she do now?" Since Mac appeared hesitant on being forthcoming with what Louise did to upset her, he thought maybe she needed a bit of prodding.

Mackenzie grabbed a handful of tissues and blew her nose, using more to dab at her eyes. A couple of additional deep breaths and she peered up at him. Her eyes and nose were bright red. Had the situation not been so dire, he would've found her appearance almost comical.

Mackenzie was never one to pussyfoot around. "Mom says you're not my real father. Tyler Channing is."

"She *what!?*" Al's cheeks flamed with indignation. He wasn't sure what to expect, but her denying him parentage to Mac was certainly not anywhere near his radar of thought.

"She's sick. It's the only thing that makes sense. She's gone mentally off her rocker. She's become so obsessed with Tyler Channing she has no inkling of what's even real anymore. She says they met once before, when he was here for a play or something. That they became intimate then and I was the result of their tryst. It's so ludicrous, and she was so adamant, I didn't even question her as to how you came into it. I'm afraid if we push her to see realty, she'll resist so hard she'll lose herself entirely. I don't know what to do!"

Al was very taken aback and had no idea what to say.

Mackenzie pulled back a bit more, dabbing at her eyes. "There's no truth to it, is there?"

"No. Of course not." But Al wasn't absolutely sure. Mac was born premature and had to remain in the hospital a couple of extra days just to keep an eye on her vitals. Al also knew Louise wasn't a virgin when they met. Hell, she practically attacked him on their second date. So now he had to wonder if she had done so because she found someone gullible in him. He hated Louise for putting these doubts in not only his mind, but also their daughter's. What was wrong with her that she'd even consider it a possibility? Why was she so intent on destroying everything they'd built up as a family? Or for that matter, the very foundations of their lives together with all her delusional lies?

Al gave a mental sigh. He'd deal with Louise later. Right now, Mackenzie needed him and he'd be here for her as long as she did.

Chapter Eight

The rapid pounding on Louise's door instantly made her think she was under attack. With a bit of nervousness, she peered through the peephole. Sighing, she opened the door. "What do you want?"

Al pushed his way in and slammed the door. Louise wasn't sure she ever remembered seeing him so furious before. The veins on his temple and neck pulsed in rapid succession.

"How dare you? Having these obsessions about Tyler Channing is one thing, but to make your daughter believe she might not be mine? That's inexcusable. Unforgivable! Why would you even do that? You need to get your head out of your ass and start living in the real world. Tyler doesn't know you, doesn't care about you, and never will. You're a nobody to him and, at best, the only thing he'll know you for now is your stalking abilities and unwillingness to leave him alone. You're spreading lies about him and yourself, and worse, you're pulling Mac and me into those delusions. Do you have any fucking clue how upset you've made her? It took her three hours before she could calm down enough to breathe. I'm lucky she didn't need to go to the hospital for anxiety."

"I only told her the truth. I've kept it from all of you long enough, but now that he's here, he's back, there's no reason to continue keeping everyone in the dark about our tryst all those years ago."

Al backhanded her across her cheek. "Snap out of it."

Louise's head snapped back. Quickly, she raised a hand to cover the rapidly spreading handprint across her skin. "How dare you? You may not like the fact that Mackenzie isn't yours or that I never disclosed that fact to anyone, but that doesn't make it any less true. I suggest you leave. Now. Or I'm calling the police."

"This isn't over, Louise. I'll see you dead before I let you propagate any further lies that'll hurt Mac." He spun on his heel and slammed the door behind him as he left, this time breaking the door jamb with the force.

Louise shook her head. She knew none of them would understand, but she'd hoped they'd try. Heading to the kitchen, she grabbed an ice pack and put it on her cheek. Shit, he'd never hit her before, but he sure knew how to find that vulnerable spot that made her whole head throb. She had to admit, though, it was the first time he scared her, and she wondered if she might've pushed him too far.

Setting the ice pack aside, Louise obtained the papers from her desk that she had retrieved last night and sat down at the kitchen table to go through them. One was an old script of *The Hoosier Schoolmaster* signed by the entire cast, including Tyler. Another was a picture of Tyler, one arm wrapped around her waist while the other was holding up a bottle of whiskey. Half the bottle was already empty. One could tell from Tyler's glazed eyes he was pretty wasted. Still, he was young, handsome and surprisingly virile for one who didn't seem sober or normal the entire time while working on the play.

He was pretty much an unknown at that period

of their lives, just getting his start in the acting business. He'd done some small parts in television and movies, even had a commercial or two before landing the role of the schoolmaster in the play.

She pulled out a stack of letters, brown with age, held together by a black ribbon. They were all addressed to Tyler, but none had ever been sent. She hadn't the nerve then. She hadn't the confidence for a lot of things back then. But age and experience have changed her hesitancy into courage. You only live once. Or as the kids now-a-days say, YOLO.

What does it matter what she does now? For when she's dead, who's going to point to any one thing she did or didn't do? Yet, she might question the decisions she made during her life when faced with a review of it.

Maybe she should've gone swimming in the ocean or taken that cruise. Maybe she should've traveled more, or taken that job when she was sixteen. Or, maybe, just maybe she should've told everyone the truth about Tyler Channing and their affair. Maybe she should've been honest long ago about Mackenzie's parentage and not tried to hide it or lie about it. However, back in her youth, she feared being an unwed mother, scared of raising a child on her own. And she knew Tyler wouldn't want to be tied down as a father when his career was just taking off.

She wouldn't hold him back in any way. Even though their time was brief, she'd fallen in love with him. She'd do anything for him. In fact, she did. She kept their affair and her pregnancy from everyone, even him, so he wouldn't feel obligated to her and not pursue his own dreams.

She was older now, wiser and far more alone than she ever recalled being in her entire life. Times had changed and so had people's views on what was socially acceptable. She no longer had to fear what others would think of her, no longer worry about the shame of being a single mother. Even letting Tyler know was no longer a concern. It was time for the truth.

Chapter Nine

Four days before the murder:

Louise checked her car. She had snacks; her camera with a powerful lens, full battery and a fresh SD card; a few things to drink; and a plastic container to use if she needed to pee. She was all set. She knew she was stalking Tyler, but she had no other choice if she was going to see him at the moment. After being arrested a couple of days ago she wasn't going to be so forthright, at least not with his family around. Thankfully, there was still the theater dressing room where she could, and would, find him alone. Time for them to be together, for him to get to know her again and all the secrets she'd carried around for years. She knew her actions would be considered a bit obsessive by some, including Al and her daughter, but they just didn't understand how patient she'd been waiting for Tyler to come back to her. They had no idea what she had gone through when he left all those years ago.

Louise jumped when her cell phone rang. So lost in her own reminisces, she was truly startled. "Hello?"

"Mom? I want you to stop dreaming about Tyler and saying those lies about him and me."

"They're not lies, Mackenzie. No matter how much you wish it so."

"Oh, my god. Mom! I can't believe you'd do this to Dad and me. He's been a good father. Why would you insult him in such a fashion?"

"Look. I'm not trying to hurt him or you. I just want you to finally know the truth. I think you deserve that. As does Tyler."

"You're so not going to spread this lie to him and his family."

"It's time he knows the truth too. Hell, maybe he'll add you to his will and you'll be wealthy. Being his daughter should have lots of perks."

"None that I want. I'm perfectly content in letting things stay as they are. Al as my dad. Tyler is some man I occasionally see grace the screen of my television."

Louise sighed. "It doesn't matter what you're willing or not willing to accept. I'm telling him the truth about you. About us."

"I'll see you dead first, Mom." Mackenzie jabbed hard at the disconnect button, almost wishing she had one of those land lines you could actually slam down the receiver she remembered as a child. She'd hoped she could reason with her mom, but Louise seemed unwavering in her deranged belief. She could only hope Louise would come to her senses before it was too late for all of them.

Closing her eyes, Mackenzie tried to catch her breath. This whole affair was just infuriating to her. When she opened them, she realized several people in the café were staring at her. Guess she hadn't been too discreet in her phone call after all. Oh, well. She was sure at one point or other they all felt the same way about their own moms.

Sighing deeply, Louise put her phone on the seat beside her. She pulled out the camera with the long telephoto lens, aiming it up to the Channing's suite. The drapes were drawn. Frowning, she put the heavy camera down and leaned back, keeping an eye on the room.

It wasn't long after when the Channing family emerged from the hotel. Surprised, she sat up, trying to remain hidden but still keeping an eye on them. Tyler was with his family and that disappointed her greatly. But she had been patient for a couple of decades now, she could continue to be so.

Bringing the camera up, she followed them, taking many, many pictures of Tyler and his family. It was nice to see him enjoying time in the city, visiting a museum, going to lunch, stopping by a couple of stores and an art exhibit before returning to their hotel.

Louise had just put in a new SD card, set her camera by the driver's window for quick access, and pulled out a sandwich to take a bite when a pounding on her window startled her, causing her to drop her sandwich all over her lap, steering wheel and onto the floor. Louise turned to find a very angry Debra standing in the middle of the street alongside her vehicle.

Rolling her window down, Louise growled, "What do you want?"

"This!" Debra reached in and grabbed the camera, throwing it on the ground so hard the lens cracked and the battery door popped open. Scooping it up, she popped out the battery, stomping on it, then removed the SD card, dropping it in a nearby puddle.

"Hey! That's my camera!"

"Maybe you should've thought of that before you used it to take pictures of us all day."

"There's no law against it. The paparazzi do it all the time."

"I don't appreciate them either, but at least they have a code of conduct I can deal with. You, on the other hand, have none." Debra threw what was left of the camera back at Louise. "I want you to stop following us and leave us alone, but somehow I don't think you're going to do that, regardless of how many times we tell you to."

"You're right. I'm not going to stay away. And nothing you say is going to make me stop. I didn't approach any of you today."

"You've been following us all day. Did you think I didn't notice you and your shitty little car trailing us everywhere we went? Did you think we hadn't spotted you with your nose pressed up against the windows of the places we stopped at today? Look, you little bitch, you're not going to come near my family again. Do you hear me? Stay the fuck away, or I'll make you wish you did. Your camera will be nothing compared to what I'll do to you."

Debra didn't give Louise a chance to respond, nor did she pay any attention to the small crowd that gathered on the sidewalk watching the exchange. She spun on her heel and headed back across the street. She was fully aware that their room could be seen from where Louise was parked and she'd make damned sure the curtains remained closed from now on.

Debra had tried to change rooms to get away

from those windows but the hotel, sadly, couldn't accommodate them. She may be stuck with the room, but she wouldn't be stuck dealing with this stalking bitch spying on them.

Chapter Ten

Three days before the murder:

Maggie's head lifted when the phone of their room rang. Not surprisingly, Tyler and Debra barely lifted their heads over the shrill sound. They both knew Maggie would handle it, as was her job. Pearl lifted her head and looked Maggie's way, though why she'd expect anyone to call her on the landline when her cell phone rarely left her hands, no one was quite sure.

"Hello?" Maggie learned long ago not to say whom she was answering for. If it was the correct line, the caller would expect Maggie to answer. If it was a wrong number, then they wouldn't know they accidently called the Channing family.

"Hello, Maggie. May I speak to Tyler, please."

"Who's calling please?"

It was quiet on the line for a few long moments. Louise debated whether giving her real name would prevent her from being put through. Biting her lip, she went with a partial lie. "Lou with wardrobe."

Maggie knew better. She knew that wardrobe was Marian, a sweet 75-year-old lady who worked out of her home and was Maggie's aunt. She was also aware of Louise Harper, who hadn't left Tyler alone since he arrived in town. "Sorry, Lou. He's unavailable at the moment. Can I take a message?"

"No. I know he's still in the room. Please put him on."

"I don't know how or why you think he's still here, but he's not. Do you wish to leave a message?"

"No. Thanks." Louise clicked the red phone symbol to disconnect. She knew he was still in the room, so it bothered her that Maggie lied.

"Who was it?" Debra asked without looking up.

Maggie threw Tyler a look, unsure if she should answer. She knew Debra was upset over their encounter a couple of nights ago at dinner with the mayor, and more so with the stalking incident yesterday. She didn't wish to cause additional problems by even mentioning the woman's name, yet she knew she had to answer Debra.

"It was that woman, Louise. Wasn't it?" Tyler knew immediately from the way Maggie was trying to protect him by hesitating in her answer.

Debra's head snapped up. "You're freaking kidding me."

Maggie sighed. "No. Mr. Channing is correct. It was Louise wanting to speak with him."

Pearl rolled her eyes. "That woman needs to get a life."

"Agreed." Debra threw her husband a dirty look.

Tyler sighed. "I'm not encouraging her in any way."

"Why is she so hung up on you?" Pearl set her cell in her lap.

Tyler shrugged. "She said we knew each other when I was here years ago for a play. Honestly, I was so drunk and high, I don't remember even being here, much less her. Still, that was ages ago. Before you were born, so I honestly don't know why she'd still be holding onto anything we *might've* had."

"She needs to get over whatever it is." Debra added silently, *unless you're lying and it's not over, which would explain so much.*

"Agreed. If I have to put out an Order of Protection against her, I will. I was hoping having her arrested the other night would've dampened her enthusiasm and get it through her head I wasn't interested." Tyler rubbed the back of his head. "Guess I was wrong."

"Guess you were," Debra snarled softly.

"I'll take care of the paperwork for you, if you wish to proceed with the order." Maggie opened her day planner, pen hoisted for notes she'd have to make.

Tyler moved to the window and looked down onto the street. The scene looked so normal as people walked up and down on their daily errands. He didn't realize the car parked across the street could easily see him standing at the window, nor that it contained Louise with binoculars, who sat watching him—waiting—her camera now destroyed.

Sighing, Tyler turned away from the window and went back over to his wife. He could see from the look on her face she wasn't happy. "Yeah. Start the paperwork. I need to have that woman leave me and mine alone. What will you need from me?"

"I'll handle it, sir. From what I understand, I'll need your signature on a few papers after I get them filled out." Maggie looked down at her day planner, then at the clock on the mantle. "You have about thirty minutes before you're due at the theater. I'll meet you there later with those papers in hand."

"That's fine." Tyler sat next to his wife. "What are you and Pearl's plans for the day?"

"Thought we would do a little shopping. I heard they have a Russian Tea Room in town, and then maybe see if we can find a spa and get our nails done. Maybe even a massage."

Pearl stood and walked in front of her dad, her hand out. "Money?"

"You do realize I'm more than just an ATM for you, right?"

"Yeah, Dad. But I also realize Mom and I need to chill after all that excitement last night, and therefore you owe us." Pearl wiggled her fingers impatiently.

Reaching into his back pocket, he pulled out his wallet and handed her his credit card. "Try not to put too much of a dent in it. We're going to be here for a few more weeks before the show even opens."

She snatched the card and stuffed it in her phone holder so fast Tyler wasn't even sure if he had it in his hand at all or if she became a magician, making it disappear with but a thought. Sometimes he felt like an enabler for their shopping habits, but another part of him was proud he could give his family the things they wanted. He pulled out keys for the rental cars Maggie made arrangements for, handing one set to Debra as he kissed her on the forehead.

A short time later, he headed into his dressing room at the theater. In a way, he was glad to be away from his family. Debra had been moody ever since that woman approached them all at dinner. He knew he'd given her cause to distrust him, but he'd been doting and loving, putting all his focus on his family and his work. He didn't want their relationship ruined over his stupidity. However, Louise was a mistake he *might* have made decades ago, before Debra even came into his life. Truthfully, he hardly remembered his time in this town, much less some woman he had a one-night stand with. Women, back then, were a dime a dozen to him. Something to keep him warm at night, but nothing more. He was young, ignorant and mindless of women's feelings. He'd grown a lot in the past couple of decades. He'd been a fool then, and his only excuse was he was still immature. It wasn't until he'd started getting paid well, got put in his place and met Debra, who straightened him out, that he pulled his head out of his ass. And still, he almost screwed that up by slipping slightly into his old habits of using women for sex. Meaningless affairs to get what Debra hadn't provided in a while. Counseling, and an adamant amendment to reform and strengthen their bonds, he continued to learn and grow. He refused to have some inconsequential sex from years ago ruin anything now. Debra, however, considered it a betrayal nonetheless, despite his arguing to the contrary.

Pulling out his cell phone, he dialed Debra's number and listened to it ring.

"Yeah."

Her snipped response told him she was still angry. "Hi. I know you and Pearl are shopping. I hope you two have fun. I was thinking, though, maybe we should set up a counseling session as soon as possible. Even if it's over the phone. I don't like the way this issue has affected us. We were on the right path and I want to continue to work on us." The idea came to him in the car as he drove over to the theater. He really did want to save his marriage and he was willing to do anything to accomplish that goal. Silence greeted him for a few moments on the phone; he wasn't sure if she was still there. "Hello? Debra?"

"I'm still here. I'm just surprised over your suggestion. I'll call Dr. Knox later and see when he can do a phone session."

Tyler's lips tweaked upward. "Perfect. Just let me know when I need to be there."

"Thank you, Tyler. Asking to work with the marriage counselor means more than I can put into words."

"Baby, you mean everything to me. I wish you'd believe that I'll do anything to make us stronger."

Debra nodded, even though she knew Tyler couldn't see it over the phone. "I'll let you know what he says after I speak with him." She hung up the phone, kicking herself that she responded so coldly when it was obvious he was making every effort to prove she meant something special to him and not to the woman who claimed they were together decades ago. It wasn't like she'd been without relationships before him. Only, her exes weren't flaunted in his face.

She looked over at Pearl as she put her phone away. "How about we pick up some lunch to go and join your father at the theater? Maybe even watch him rehearse for a bit?"

Pearl looked up from examining her fingernails being worked on by the manicurist and smiled. "That sounds like a great idea. I'm sure he'd love it." She was glad when the two of them spent time together. Like most kids, she wanted her parents to be happy together and she knew they'd been having a rough time of it lately. She didn't know what the phone call was about, but it seemed to put her mom in a much happier mood. "I saw a deli just down the street. We can get him a roast beef sandwich. I know he'll love that."

"Sounds like a plan. We'll get something once we finish here." Debra leaned back into the massaging chair while her feet soaked in the tub and her own nails were being worked on. While they waited for their lunch to be made, she'd call the counselor and set up an appointment.

Chapter Eleven

Maggie left Tyler's dressing room, notes in hand of things she needed to handle for him. Mostly it was responding to some mail that had finally found its way from being forwarded from their California residence. She also had some emails to reply to on Tyler's behalf and a couple of personal errands to do for the family. Being Tyler's personal assistant certainly kept her busy, but he also knew she was from Moraine Valley, the small township just outside of Valley View, and tried to give her some time to visit old friends and family.

As she closed the door and started to walk away, she almost tripped on a basket on the ground. She frowned as she picked it up to see if there was any information on whom it might be from. Her concern was that it was from Louise Harper, who had done nothing but make herself a total nuisance to the Channing Family.

There was no note or any other indication of who brought the basket to him, and it contained fruit, muffins and chocolate. Shrugging, she tapped lightly on the door and peeked her head inside. "Sorry to bother you, but there was a basket left outside for you. No note, so maybe from the theater staff?"

Tyler looked up from his script, his reading glasses on the tip of his nose, and he looked over the rims at her. "Fine, fine. Just set it over there. I noticed I had a couple of bouquets of flowers too. One was from the management and another was from the author of the play, Kendall Falcon. I'm sure you're correct and these are more of the same. Albeit, I do enjoy muffins. Pearl will like the chocolate and Debra will love the fruit. It's very generous they're making us feel so welcomed."

"I'm glad, especially after the not-so-enjoyable presence you seem to have attracted since you arrived."

"Do you know her at all?" He pulled his glasses off entirely, giving Maggie his full attention.

"I'm not sure. She's a bit younger than me. About your age, I believe. So I wouldn't have been in her peer circles growing up. And I've been gone from the area now for about thirty years. Sorry."

"No. It's my fault for having assumed you just knew everyone." He chuckled softly as he played with his glasses, twirling them around by the end of one of the arms.

Maggie smiled. "Sadly, though Moraine Valley is small, neighboring Valley View is quite a metropolis for this area."

"You can put the basket over there." He pointed to a small table by a couch near the door.

Maggie nodded, placing the elaborate gift where he designated and opened the door. "I'll get those errands done for you. Are you sure you don't want me to pick you up something for lunch?"

"Not really hungry, Mags. But thanks." He slipped the glasses on his nose and turned back to the script, red pen in hand, hearing the door close as Maggie slipped out, trying to be as unobtrusive as possible. That was something he really liked about her. Not only was she ever so efficient, she tried to be invisible as much as possible.

It wasn't but a couple of moments when he heard the door open again. "Did you forget something?" He turned around in his chair, but became instantly furious as he recognized his visitor. "What are you doing here? Get out now or I'll physically throw you out. I'm not interested."

Louise waved her hand at him in a shushing manner. "Calm down. I'm not going to rape you or anything. I just wanted to show you a couple of things, then I'll leave you alone."

"I'm not interested in anything you want to show me. Please leave. This is the last time I ask nicely."

"Behave, Tyler. I'm not going to kill you. Here. Look at these."

She thrust out a stack of papers to him. On top was a picture of a slightly drunk, younger Tyler surrounded by a group on a stage, his arm wrapped around a young, beautiful woman with long brunette hair. He could tell, after a moment, that the beautiful woman was Louise when she was younger, before age and everyday living took its toll on her youthful features. He didn't bother to look at the other items in the small stack she had thrust at him as he tried to hand them back. "Okay. Look. I was pretty wild then, and drunk off my ass most of the time. I barely remember being here for that show and I, sadly, don't remember you at all. It's been many years and I've moved on with my life, straightened up. I have a loving family and I'm just not interested in you. I am sorry. I know it probably feels like I've led you on or something, but after so many years, do you really think I've had any feelings for you? Trust me, if I had, I would've been in contact with you at some point or other during those years. Now, please, take your things and go."

Louise didn't move, didn't take the papers back, but shook her head instead. "No. There's more to those papers and pictures than just that. These are only copies of the originals, so it won't matter if you destroy them. I'm not a fool, Tyler. I know you've sobered up and how difficult it was. That you spent time in rehab, though no one was supposed to know. Shortly after, that's when you met your wife. I know everything. But I want you to know a couple of things too."

"Like what? What could you possibly have to tell me that I'd have any interest in knowing?"

"How about that I got pregnant from our time together?"

Tyler grabbed her arm in a vise-like grip so hard they both knew it was going to leave bruises behind, but he didn't care if she filed for abuse or not. The bitch was crazy. "Nice try." He started to drag her towards the door.

Louise twisted out of his grip, then used her fingertip to poke at the center of his chest. "Look. Look at the pictures. Look at the papers. You've got a kid in this world that you didn't even know about. You may want to pretend it didn't happen, or say you forgot about me or didn't care, but for three weeks we were close. Intimate. And you left me with something—no, someone—to remember our time together. It's about time you know about her as well. Look."

Tyler brought the papers up again, but he didn't

really look through them, just the top picture of the two of them again. He tossed the papers aside. "I don't care. Even if it's true, I don't care. You're not going to blackmail me for money. It was a long time ago, before I met Debra or had a family. No one is going to care." He grabbed her arm but she swung around, so he grabbed the other arm as well in order to prevent her from pressing closer to him.

"I don't want your money. *We* have a child. She's done nothing to you. What would it hurt to meet her? Get to know her?" Louise was going to continue but stopped when she heard a gasp behind her.

Tyler looked up at the sound as well, dropping his hands, a guilty expression on his face. "Debra. It's not what it seems."

Debra stormed in, pushing Louise away from Tyler and addressing her husband. "Not what it seems? You have a child with this woman? How could you? How could you do this to us? To me? To Pearl?"

Pearl stood in the entryway holding a couple of

white bags with the words Kelli's Deli imprinted on them. She was pale, trembling slightly, visibly upset, but remained quiet. She knew this was something her parents would have to deal with. She turned her attention and glared at Louise, hating the woman who caused a rift between her mother and father.

"I wasn't doing anything. Debra, calm down." Tyler took a firm stand with his wife.

"Not doing anything? You were holding her in your arms. Talking about having a kid between you two. How is that not doing anything? Look, don't worry about us. Pearl and I are leaving. We came to bring you lunch, but that was a huge mistake. We're done." Debra turned on her heel and stormed out of the dressing room, grabbing Pearl to drag with her. She snatched the paper deli bag out of her hands and tossed it to Tyler, not caring that it hit him in the shoulder but wishing there was a can of soda or something else that would've made a harder impact.

Louise shifted uncomfortably, having watched the whole exchange. A part of her was dancing on the inside. With Debra gone, Louise would have a better chance to be with Tyler. She'd be the shoulder he could cry on if need be. She'd make him forget his wife.

Tyler didn't care about being hit with the bag. He ran to the door, but Debra and Pearl were already out of the theater. He spun angrily. "If I ever see you again, I'll kill you. Get out of my dressing room and out of my life." He turned again and headed out to the manager's office. Security would have to be upgraded if they wanted him to stay. He'd also have Maggie make sure she got all the papers she'd need to file for the Order of Protection against Louise. He was done trying to placate her by being nice. Louise might've screwed up his opportunity to fix things with his wife, and he'd never forgive her for that. He felt he probably left Louise standing there in shock, but he didn't care. She needed to go home and leave him the fuck alone while he tried to calm down and deal with his irate wife and his collapsing marriage.

Chapter Twelve

Two days before the murder:

It took Tyler a long time to convince Debra he was telling the truth. He'd had security tightened at the theater; he'd threatened Byron of leaving if he hadn't. Byron, thankfully, had overheard some of the argument and came to see what was occurring when Debra and Pearl arrived yesterday, but then ducked back into his office once the two women stormed away.

Byron hated spending money on additional security, but if he wanted the headliner of Tyler Channing, he'd have to spend a little in order for the big rewards at the box office later on. Tyler refused to step one foot in the theater until Byron could guarantee it was safe from Louise or anyone else who tried to invade his privacy.

Byron greeted Tyler at the door, shaking the man's hand. "I'm glad you came back."

"Your phone call this morning said you got more security, which is what I'd asked for."

"I did. We have all the other doors but the backstage one locked from the inside, and that one will be manned, as you noticed when you came in, 24/7 by Guardian Security Company. They employ mostly off-duty or retired officers and ex-military. No one, especially some woman, is going to get past them."

"Thank you. I'm sorry it's come to this, but I didn't know what else to do to stop that woman from bothering me and my family. We even filed for an Order of Protection against her yesterday. I'm told she will be served today. Hopefully she'll take it seriously enough to leave me and mine alone."

"I know Louise. She's a friend of Kendall's, the writer. As a matter of fact, she was Kendall's matron of honor at her wedding just a couple of weeks ago. I'd never seen Louise as anything other than a kindly woman who had a bit of motherly affection for everyone. Although, I admit, the past few months she'd become a bit of a recluse. I'm not sure what happened to change her."

"I don't know either, but motherly affection is not what she has for me and I don't care for her trying to get me to be with her. It's a strain on my wife too."

"I am sorry about all of it, but you can bet your bottom dollar she's not stepping in this theater, even if she buys a dozen tickets."

Tyler chuckled. "Well, I certainly couldn't ask for more than that. Thank you."

"You're welcome."

"What time does Mrs. Falcon arrive? I'd like to go through my notes with her before we really start with rehearsals."

"She'll be here at one. Ms. Marian Keeler will be here in about an hour to get your measurements for costume fittings."

"Ah, yes. I've been looking forward to meeting with her. She's my P.A.'s aunt and I've heard only wonderful things about her from Mags."

"That's right. I'd almost forgotten. Ms. Marian is a bit older, but she's been an institution here at the theater, doing all of our costumes for the past fifty years, and she's extremely talented. Out of respect for her, we call her Ms. Marian."

"Wonderful. Send her to my room when she arrives. I'm going to go over the script one more time in preparation of my meeting with Mrs. Falcon."

"Just a tip, she isn't used to the Mrs. part yet, so you might want to address her as Kendall. We're all pretty informal around here."

"I'll keep that in mind, Byron. Later." Tyler nodded as he left the room, walking down the corridors to his private dressing room. He passed a few of the stagehands and took a moment to speak with each one, if for nothing else other than salutations and introductions.

He'd finally made it to his dressing room and closed the door with a sigh of relief. A bit of his introversions had begun to surface, and he was grateful for a moment of peace and solitude. He noticed a few things left from yesterday's encounter. The first was a basket brought in from Maggie. He checked it out to see if there was a note, hoping it was from the theater management or something, but no note could be found. He debated, then picked up the entire basket and dropped it in the trash. He wasn't about to take any chances it was from Louise Harper because he wanted nothing from that woman other than to have her leave him alone.

He grabbed the script and haphazardly collapsed on the couch to run through it yet again. It was only as he lay there that he heard paper rustling under him. Sitting up, he pulled out a stack of papers to see what they were.

They were typed and appeared as a communication between someone named Lucas and Lily. It started out as the two of them meeting for some café au lait and beignets at the Café du Monde in New Orleans. As Tyler skimmed it, he was surprised at how sexually explicit it had become and eventually he had to stop reading. He had no idea where it came from or who left it, but then remembered Louise had a bunch of papers in her hand, along with a couple of pictures. Still, he wasn't sure what Lily and Lucas had to do with Louise or him. And then he saw it. One of the first pages showed pictures of Lucas and they were his face staring back at him. What the hell? Why was Lucas using Tyler's face as a profile picture? More of Louise's lies, he supposed. For all he knew, Louise was Lily, although the face of the profile was not that of Louise. Instead, it looked more like Keira Knightley.

Shaking his head, he tossed the entire set of papers into the trashcan. A couple of pictures fell from between the pages. Scooping to pick them up, he couldn't help but glance at them. One he'd already seen, that of a younger him with a younger Louise. Another showed a young teenager with the same hazel eyes he had. Could it be the daughter Louise said he fathered? Just because they had the same color eyes didn't mean he was the father, but he had to admit, they were strikingly similar to his own. She was a pretty young girl. The next was the same girl, but older and more mature with the same piercing eyes.

Great! Now I'm letting Louise make me doubt my belief that I couldn't possibly have conceived a child with her.

His thoughts were interrupted by a knock on the door. He'd managed to get nothing done before Ms. Marian arrived to get his measurements for wardrobe. He tossed the pictures in the trash bin on top of everything else already there and went to let Maggie's aunt in.

Chapter Thirteen

Present Day:

Detective Caleb Mitchell looked at the crime scene. He had on his plastic gloves and paper booties so as not to contaminate the area. The body had already been removed to the morgue for a full autopsy, albeit, they were pretty sure they knew what the cause of death was, even if they hadn't found the murder weapon yet. Hard for anyone to survive being stabbed in the eye and neck several times. Though with what weapon, he'd have to wait for the coroner's official report. The coroner was able to confirm time of death due to the lividity of the body, indicating she'd been dead for about fourteen to fifteen hours, since about nine or ten last night. He'd have to check the alibis of his potential suspects for last night. In the meantime, he had forensics combing the building, but he was also taking a look to get clues as to who might have murdered Louise Harper and why. As he walked around, examining all of the markers placed earlier, he tried to imagine what had occurred.

To him, it appeared the murder itself wasn't planned. However, a random act was more dangerous and harder to solve, as far as he was concerned. It meant Louise knew her murderer enough to let them in and, from all appearances, had a brief social hour. There were two wine glasses on the table and a plate of cheeses. One empty wine bottle was tossed in the trash. A full, unopened bottle was lying slightly under the couch, as if dropped and having rolled to that position. He looked at the wine glasses a bit closer. Neither had lipstick on them, but both should have some DNA. Of course, one of them would be Mrs. Harper's. It only made sense the other would be the assailant.

"Mark," Caleb called to Officer Simon, who was taking pictures of the crime scene. "Make sure you get these glasses down to the lab for DNA analysis. There's also a couple of napkins, probably used for the cheese nearby. Get those too."

"Sure thing." Mark reached into the small duffle he had on his shoulder to pull out an evidence kit. Using the bags inside out, he secured the items, writing on each of them where they were located and the case number, so the lab wouldn't get them confused with another case accidently.

Caleb noticed a tip of white paper sticking out from under a La-Z-Boy recliner. He scooped it up but was disappointed in it just being a corner from a torn picture. Feeling it was important, he placed the corner in an evidence bag and began to look around for more of the picture. He couldn't help but wonder if it'd been burned in the fireplace, as there was a pretty decent pile of ashes. He poked around them a bit before he decided to let the officers go through it more efficiently and tag anything of value they might find. Frowning, he looked around the room again and knew what it was that was bothering him since he walked in.

"Mark, keep a look out for more pieces of this torn picture or any pictures whatsoever. For a woman who's married and has a daughter, there don't seem to be any family photos about. Dillion," Caleb called to Officer Dillion Davies, "collect all the papers you can find. I'll go through them at the office. Make sure you get all the letters and financials, as well as anything that might be recognizable from the fire. And don't forget to grab the laptop and get it to tech. I'd like to see if she had any email threats or anything else that might be of use to the investigation. Tell them to put a stat on it as well. I don't want to be waiting months for them to get access."

"Yes, sir," Dillion called back. He'd already been putting everything in collection bags before putting the bags in file boxes to be brought to the station. He made a mental note to check the upstairs for the computer, because it hadn't been located on the main floor.

"I find it very odd there are no photos on the wall or mantle. Did you find any photos in any other rooms?"

"We haven't had a chance to go through all of them yet. Just the downstairs and a quick glance upstairs to make sure the house was clear of intruders."

"Alright. Photograph and record everything." Caleb knew the two of them would be busy most of the day packing up possible evidence and getting clues. Looking around a bit more, he was about to admit defeat in finding the rest of the picture when he noticed something stuck in the cushions of the couch. Pulling on it, he realized he'd found two more pieces. He could see a young woman and the body of a man. The face was missing, but on the limb around the waist of the woman was a visible tattoo of cannabis leaves on the forearm. Shouldn't be too difficult to find. He added the pieces into the bag of the original corner he'd found earlier. His instincts told him that picture would be his biggest clue in finding the person who killed Louise Harper.

"I think I found it, sir," Mark called, gaining Caleb's attention.

Caleb rapidly joined him to look behind the pulled-out bureau, used as a beverage area on top, holding several bottles of liquor. Looking around Mark, Caleb could see the item. His stomach churned slightly, noticing all the blood caked upon it. "You're probably right. The coroner will have to confirm it, but from what I saw of the body, this is probably the murder weapon. Bag the corkscrew and send it to the lab, along with everything else."

The attack on Louise had been totally vicious, and circumstances made him believe it wasn't planned in advance. It was a crime of opportunity. A lot of murderers, even if they were known by the victim, would come in and do the job right away, then leave immediately. This one took the time to socialize, drinking wine and having cheese. So, what went wrong? Did it have something to do with the picture torn in pieces? Or something else? The house had been ransacked, as if looking for something. What had they been searching for? Did they find it? Questions raced through his mind as he tried to figure out what happened and how. He knew it would only be a careful, long and exhaustive investigation that would provide the answers he sought, but it always helped to get some background to start with.

He glanced at his watch. He'd been here for a

couple of hours already. He knew the victim's daughter was taken to the station and he did want to speak to her, so he left a few verbal notes with the officers and headed to the department.

The police department was attached to the Village Hall, albeit they had separate entrances and interiors. The detectives' offices were down in the basement, but they were large and roomy with lots of smaller rooms for the labs and autopsies. It was nice to have everything in one space, even if the building took up a whole city block. Miss Harper would be waiting for him up on the first floor in the interrogation room. He knew she'd been waiting awhile, but it couldn't be helped. Besides, he was sure she needed some alone time to process her grief. He knew one of the other officers would've brought her some water. He doubted if she wanted or needed anything else from the description Mark gave of how distraught she was when she learned of her mother's demise.

The picture fragment still bothered him. He pulled the pieces from the bag and taped them up.

He would show Miss Harper the picture and see if she knew who the woman was or who had that tattoo on his arm. Hopefully she could give him some idea as to who might want to hurt her mother and set him on his path for his investigation. It would be a few days before the labs got back to him. Thankfully, Valley View only had their own cases and those of major importance to Moraine Valley, so getting the autopsy report, even if it was just the preliminary, shouldn't take more than twenty-four hours.

In the meantime, it was time to start the interrogation of Miss Harper.

Chapter Fourteen

Caleb put everything he was going to need in a file folder, checked that he had a small voice recorder and a notepad and pen for notes he wanted to make, and made sure the interrogation room was recording. He tapped lightly on the door to inform Miss Harper someone was about to enter, so as not to startle her. When he entered the room, he stopped short, his breath catching in his throat. "Mackenzie?"

She looked up as the door opened and gasped. It didn't take but a moment for her to recognize him as the man she had met at the wedding a couple of weeks ago and thought never to see again after she ran out after her mother. She'd meant to get his number or give him hers, but she hadn't expected her parents to have a complete breakdown and not return to the reception until it was too late, having to deal with her father slashing her mother's tires. She didn't even know his last name or where he worked. Until now. Now he was standing in the police interrogation room with a folder, a voice recorder, and a look of total astonishment on his face. Guess he never thought he'd see her again either. And certainly not under these conditions.

He quickly regained his composure and stoically entered the room. "I hadn't realized Louise Harper was your mother. My condolences." He slipped into the chair opposite from her, pushing forward a box of tissues. He could tell from her reddened eyes and nose she'd been crying most of the time she'd been sitting there.

Mackenzie didn't waste any time grabbing another tissue from the box, though she twisted it in her hands more than used it for her eyes or nose. "Thanks. I can't believe it. Why would anyone want her dead?"

"I was kinda hoping you'd answer that. Has everything been okay with your mom of late? What about your parents in general? I know there were some issues at the wedding."

"Yeah. They are—were getting a divorce, but only because she wanted it. I'm pretty sure Dad wanted to stay with her."

"Why did she want the divorce?"

"A couple of reasons. If you ask Dad, he'll tell you mostly 'cause she's been a bit crazy of late."

"What do you mean?"

"Well, about a year ago or so she got hooked on this role-play game on the computer. She'd spend almost every waking minute on there playing with someone."

"Role-playing? What's that?"

"Well, you know, on Facebook you have a post and people post responses underneath? Well, same thing, mostly. Only with role-play, you create a character, choose an avatar and write make-believe scenes that someone responds to while playing this game of fantasy. I don't really understand it much. I tried when Mom first started this game. It centers around a set of books she reads. The characters, at least. Anyways, Mom became so involved, nothing else existed, especially Dad. They fought constantly about it and, finally, he gave up and moved out. She filed for divorce almost immediately afterward."

"Do you think your father could've done this?"

"No." She responded without hesitation. "Dad is more patient than he should be. He doesn't have a mean bone in his body. Sure, he gets angry, but it's only because of how she was shutting him out."

"I remember your mother coming in, frantically stating her tires were cut by your father. He sounds like he could get pretty angry, and even violent, to me."

"Maybe, but Mom was pushing his buttons lately. He's human. He gets angry. He might've even made threats, but that's all they would've been. He's patient, but he's not a saint. He'd never hurt a person. I know he could never hurt her, much less kill her. It's not in him." Mackenzie rubbed her hands together in a nervous fashion.

Caleb jotted down a couple of things he wanted to check on later, like the background of the others that captured Louise's interest as part of this game she played online.

"Can you think of anyone else who might wish your mom dead?"

Mackenzie paused, trying desperately to think about the question and going through the list of people her mother knew. "How could I be so stupid? I guess with the shock of everything, and I'm sure it doesn't mean anything, but she was arrested a couple of nights ago."

"Arrested? For what?"

"Um. I can't remember all the charges. Disorderly conduct, harassment, causing a disturbance, resisting arrest. I'm not exactly sure." Mackenzie rubbed her temple.

"You said this happened when?"

"A week ago."

"So, last Sunday?"

"Yes. I remember I had to go to work the next day and it was late by the time we got her bailed out."

"Excuse me a moment." Caleb headed out of the room and went to the desk clerk's office. "Sally? Can you check the calls for an arrest of Louise Harper last Sunday night?"

Sally smiled. She liked when the officers gave

her things to look up. It helped to keep her busy and she enjoyed that part of her job. "Sure thing." She stood and grabbed the lockup log and opened it, scanning for Louise's name. "Ah, here it is. Case number 78243901." She jotted the number down and returned to the computer to pull up the arrest report and notes. She then printed out a copy and handed Caleb the report.

"Thanks." He quickly scanned the report and noticed a couple of names that surprised him.

"Welcome," she called after him as he headed back to the interrogation room.

Tucking the report in his folder, he reentered the room. "Sorry about that. I wanted to see what had occurred."

"It's okay. I only remember that I came with Dad, when I got the call she'd been arrested, to bring the bail money."

"How does she know Tyler Channing?"

"She says she met him years ago, although I'm unsure of how true that actually is. Her role-play partner uses his pictures as his avatar for his profile in their games. I think she might've just gotten confused between that and actually knowing him. He doesn't seem to know her. I heard his family was putting out an Order of Protection against her to keep her away from them."

"He's only been in town for, what now, a week?"

She shrugged her shoulders. "Something like that. I really haven't paid much attention to his comings and goings."

"What about her role-play partner? Do you think he might know Louise? Do you think he might be jealous of the attention she was giving to Mr. Channing?"

Mackenzie shrugged her shoulders. "I don't know him at all or how much of Mom's real life he was aware of."

Caleb rifled through the folder and pulled out the torn picture he'd found in the house. "Do you know who these people are?"

Mackenzie took the photo and examined it. "That's Mom, when she was younger. I'd say about twenty or twenty-five years ago, maybe?"

"Do you recognize the tattoo?"

She stared at it for a long time, then shook her head. "No. Sorry."

"That's okay. It was a long shot." Caleb put the picture back in the folder just as there was a knock on the door. "Excuse me."

He quickly stepped outside to find Officer Simon there. "What do you have for me?"

Mark held out a stack of crime scene pictures. "I thought you should see this. It was in a spare bedroom."

Taking the pictures, Caleb frowned.

"We also found some anti-depressants and anti-psychotics in her medicine cabinet."

"Check with the doctor on the labels and see if you can get what her diagnosis was that caused these medications to be prescribed. And when she started them. This might explain the psycho room here." He waved the pictures in the air.

"You having any luck with her daughter in figuring out who the culprit is?" Mark tilted his head to indicate the interrogation room.

"I thought it might be the husband, but with this, the list just went up tenfold. Let me know when you found out something. Thanks."

Caleb shook his head. Louise seemed to have far more mental problems than anyone seemed to realize. Or did they? Returning to his seat in the interrogation room, he decided to play it cool and see what she would admit to knowing.

"Was your mother on any medications?"

"Sure. She was on some blood pressure meds, and I think some water pills to help with the swelling she had in her feet."

"Anything else?"

Mackenzie shook her head. "No. Not that I'm aware of."

"You don't live there, do you?"

"No. I have my own place in Moraine Valley."

"When did you move out there?"

"About three years ago. It's closer to my work."

"What do you do?"

"I'm a secretary for a real estate company. Landers and Krane."

"How did you get along with your mom?"

"Overall, as well as could be expected. We had our little disagreements, but nothing that wouldn't blow over in a bit."

"What about how she was with Tyler Channing?"

Mackenzie shook her head. "She's so hung up on him she can't see reason, or listen to it either. I tried talking to her about the person versus the avatar, but she wouldn't listen. Not to me or to anyone."

"Did you know she continued to pursue Mr. Channing even after she was arrested? And long before he even came to town?"

"I knew she'd been into Tyler ever since she started on Facebook. Role-playing is all she talked about since she got that computer. And Lucas, the character she played with, is all she wanted."

"Lucas is the one who used Tyler as an avatar?"

"Yes."

He jotted down a note to make sure the tech department checked for an IP address for whoever played Lucas with Louise. "Did you know about this?" He laid five pictures across the table in front of her.

Mackenzie's eyes widened in horror. "No. I knew she had a thing for Tyler Channing, but nothing like this."

All five pictures were of a room that was like a shrine to Tyler Channing. Pictures, posters, newspaper clippings. Most disturbing were the boards she had covered with pictures of Tyler and his family from various locations about town. It was obvious they hadn't known she was taking their pictures, albeit, most of them were of Tyler himself. There were pictures of him standing by the window of his hotel room, getting in and out of vehicles, talking to the manager at the theater in the office or while on stage. It was really creepy: all the stalking Louise obviously did in order to obtain these photographs.

Mackenzie rubbed her stomach. The idea that her mother was so infatuated with Tyler that she'd go to these lengths just to see him unnerved her beyond words. Heaven only knew what else Louise might have done to get close to Tyler. Mackenzie had no idea her mother had gone off the deep end. Getting arrested was only one result. If things had kept going as they obviously were, lord only knew how they'd end up for Tyler and his family.

"I'm sorry." Caleb reached his hand across, patting Mackenzie's free hand. "I know this isn't easy for you."

"I just had no idea. It almost seems unreal. This wasn't the woman who was my mother. Who raised me. This wasn't the woman who was a dedicated wife all my life. This...person who took all these pictures is a stranger to me. I honestly don't know who this person is, but it's not my mother."

"I hate to ask this, but I have to. Where were you last night about 9pm?"

"I understand. You have to ask in order to clear me from your suspect list. Only I don't have much of an alibi. I was at home watching television."

"Alone?"

"Yes."

"What did you watch?"

"I was catching up on *The Walking Dead*. I'm about two seasons behind, so I was streaming it on Netflix."

"I'd like access to your account so we can verify that you were streaming the shows."

"Sure. I'll write it down for you." She waited until he passed her a pad of paper and a pen and she wrote down her account information. Although she knew as well as he did that she could have set up the show to run and left the house. Yep, she had a pretty weak alibi, but whoever really thinks they are going to need one? She silently passed the pad back to him.

"I guess that's all for now. I might have more questions for you later on."

"No problem. I'm more than happy to answer anything you need, just so long as you find who killed my mom."

Caleb nodded, helping her out of the chair. He so desperately wanted to ask her to dinner later that night, but she was now part of a serious investigation and it wouldn't be very professional if he went on a date with a suspect. He only prayed she was innocent of the dastardly deed.

"I'm going to have Officer Davies take you back in order to get your car. Do you feel okay to drive after he returns you to your vehicle?"

"Yes. I'm only going to go a few blocks to my dad's place anyway. I don't even know if anyone else knows what happened."

"We had an officer go over there to inform him. I'm sure he's let the rest of your family and friends know." Caleb pulled a business card out of his jacket's breast pocket. "If you think of anything, or if you just need to talk, call me. Anytime."

"Thank you, Detective." She took the card and put it in her purse. "By the way, the officers wouldn't let me see her. How? I mean, how was she killed?"

"We'll have to wait for the autopsy to make the

final report."

"Was she shot?"

"No. She was stabbed."

"In the chest? Or someplace where she suffered as she bled out?"

"She didn't suffer, Mackenzie." He sighed. She might as well know the truth. "She was stabbed in her head. I'm sure death was instantaneous."

She dabbed at her eyes. "At least there's that. When will we be able to go through her things?"

"Not for a while. The whole house is a crime scene at the moment."

"Of course. I understand. Thank you, Detective."

"Caleb, please. If you need anything, please don't hesitate to call on me."

"Just let me know updates on the case and find the bastard who killed her."

Caleb nodded as he showed her to the waiting room while Officer Davies was called to drive her back to her vehicle. As much as he liked Mackenzie, he couldn't help but wonder if she was the killer. After all, she seemed to be in a rush to get back into the house, and he'd been told the officers had to physically restrain her from entering the building once she found out her mother was deceased. Was she hoping to get in there to get rid of evidence she might have accidently left behind? Or something else? Only time would tell.

Chapter Fifteen

Caleb watched Davies leave with Mackenzie in the backseat of a squad car. "Damn." He turned away as he headed for his own car. He needed to interview Al Harper. He'd prefer to do it before Mackenzie arrived at her dad's place. He could avoid the whole issue by having Al brought in, but he wanted to see the apartment Al currently lived in. Seeing where a man resided could be very telling with regards to a man's thought processes. If he was living spartanly, then he planned on eventually returning home. Extravagantly, he anticipated on coming into wealth quickly, like maybe part of an insurance policy. Anything in between could still be informative as to Al's mindset. Caleb also knew if suspects remained in their own place when being questioned, they tended to be more comfortable, thinking they could pull the wool over a detective's eyes better and get away with more, which usually led to them spilling something important to the case.

Caleb headed directly to the address he had for Al. Once he was on Mr. Harper's doorstep, he straightened his tie and buttoned his suit jacket, then rang the bell. It was only moments before he heard the heavy footsteps of someone's approach and the door opened immediately after.

"Yes?" Al squinted at Caleb questioningly.

"Hello, Mr. Harper?"

"That's me. Can I help you?"

Caleb pulled out his badge. "Detective Mitchell. I'm investigating the death of Louise Harper."

"Oh. Um. Yeah. Come on in." Al stepped back to allow Caleb to enter the apartment. He ushered him into the kitchen from the foyer as he shut the front door. "One of your officers stopped by earlier with the news. He said Mac, my daughter, found her? Would you like some coffee?"

"That'd be very nice. Thank you. Yes, Mackenzie was the one who called in a well-being check on her mother and met the officers to let them in. It was the officers who found the body. They kept Mackenzie outside, so she didn't actually see her mother."

"Was it bad?"

Caleb paused, pulling the mug of joe to him as he sat at the kitchen table. "Yeah. It was pretty bad."

"Then I'm glad she didn't see her mother. No one should have to remember someone they loved in such a bad way. Better to remember her in a good way." Al sat down across from him, a coffee mug to the side, next to an ashtray filled with cigarette butts and a box of smokes nearby. A phone book also lay near the other items, the book opened to the F section.

"Where were you last night?"

Al blinked. "What? Last night? Do you think I did it?"

Caleb gave a slight shrug. "It's a standard question. We have to eliminate as many suspects as we can in order to find the murderer."

"Yes. Of course. Let's see. Last night? Well, I was here. Alone."

"What were you doing?"

"Reading. I'm not much for television other than the news, but I do enjoy literature."

"Oh? What are you reading? Anything good?"

"It was okay. Actually, I was catching up on some magazines. Not a book. Guns and Ammo and a fishing one. I don't remember at this time."

Caleb remained stoic, though inside his eyebrow went up in question. How can you not remember what you were reading less than twenty-four hours ago? And his story changed from literature to magazines.

"Do you have any clues as to who might have done this to my wife?"

"I thought you were separated and getting a divorce?"

Al shrugged and lit up another cigarette as he leaned back in his chair. "We were separated, but as for the divorce? We were trying to get back together."

"That's not what I heard. She had served papers on you just a couple of weeks ago."

"Yeah. She did, but I never signed them. We were going to work it out."

"Work what out?"

"Our problems."

"Which were?"

Al remained quiet, inhaling the nicotine deeply.

Caleb watched him closely. He appeared nervous and jittery, and the detective wondered what the man was concerned about. "Would it possibly have anything to do with Tyler Channing?"

Al's face darkened in anger. "Louise has nothing to do with that man. She's gone off the deep end thinking that someone so good looking and famous would ever want to be with someone the likes of her."

"So you think she didn't actually know Tyler Channing?"

"Oh, she met him alright. Had to bail her ass out of jail just last week. Arrested for harassment. Heard she was served a couple of days ago with an Order of Protection to stay away from him and his family."

"When's the last time you saw or talked to Louise?"

"Two days ago, when she got served. She called me up accusing me of having something to do with keeping her away from Tyler. She just couldn't understand she'd made a nuisance of herself with him or that he wanted nothing to do with her."

"Did you see her then?"

"No. The last time I saw her was a couple of days after her arrest. Mac went over to see her, and Louise upset her so much Mac came here. After I got her calmed down enough, I went over to give Louise a piece of my mind. I told her she needed to stop living in some fantasy world or she'd lose not only me, but Mac too."

"How did Louise take that?"

Al snorted, then drew in some more smoke. "She didn't like that I told her the truth about things. She yelled at me. I admit I slapped her face. Only to try and snap her out of it, you know. She's my wife and I wasn't about to give up on that, or her. We'd been together for a long time. I wasn't about to let her just throw everything away for her silliness."

"Do you know if she was on any medication?"

Al flicked his ashes into the tray. "Some blood pressure, I think."

"That the only thing?"

"I don't really keep up on her medical health."

Caleb nodded. "Of course. You were separated." It was a bit of a gibe, but he couldn't resist. If you actually loved someone, wouldn't you want to know everything about them, including their health and what medicines they were on? Maybe it was the detective in him, but he figured everyone in love would want to know all those intimate things about the person they were involved with.

"Yeah. Separated. So, when can we get her back to bury her?"

"It won't be for a while. We have the autopsy and labs to do before she can be released for burial."

"And her stuff? When can we get into the house and take care of her things?"

That's the second family member to worry about getting into the house, and Caleb actually lifted a single eyebrow in consternation. "It's a crime scene, so that, too, will be a while. We'll inform you and your daughter when everything has been released."

"Fine, fine."

"Who do you think might wish ill-will towards Louise? Enough to see her dead, that is?"

Al shrugged as he drew in another breath from the cigarette. "No one I can think of. Although, I'm sure Tyler wasn't too thrilled with her. Not sure if it was enough to see her dead, though."

"I've heard a rumor that Louise was telling others you weren't Mackenzie's father, but Tyler was."

Al slammed his fist on the table, rattling everything on it and spilling Caleb's untouched coffee. "That's a bunch of crap. Mac is my daughter, and no one is going to say otherwise," he snarled threateningly.

"Not even Louise?"

"Not even her. Mac doesn't need those lies being spread about her and me. Look. Louise was once a kind, loving mother and wife. I bought her a Christmas gift a couple years ago of a computer. Worse thing I'd ever done. She got hooked on Facebook and her whole personality suffered as a result. She went bonkers. Mixed up real life with her fantasies. She was sick in the head. I'd've slapped some sense into her if I thought it would've done any good. Maybe you should talk to Tyler and his family. They weren't thrilled with her delusions any more than Mac and I were."

"How do you know that?"

"'Cause they wouldn't've had her arrested or served her with papers to stay away from him."

Caleb pulled out his notepad and jotted down a couple of things he hadn't wanted to forget. "Do you think Louise could've been on something for her moods?"

"I don't know. If she wasn't, she should've

been."

"Thank you for your time, Mr. Harper. I might have more questions for you in a bit, but this will suffice for the time being." Caleb stood and held his hand out to shake Al's hand.

Al followed suit in standing, shook his hand and led the detective to the door. "Let me know when the body and her place are released. I still have some things there and would like to move back into the home I actually paid for."

"I will, sir. Thank you for your time."

Caleb had just gotten into his vehicle when Mackenzie pulled up. He watched as she got out of her car and rang the bell. Al opened it and the two hugged tightly before Al brought her into his abode. Al took a guilty look around before he shut the door. Caleb found the whole incident odd and it piqued his curiosity.

The interview with Al also brought about a lot of other questions, some of which he knew he'd only get answers from one person: his next interview. Tyler Channing.

Chapter Sixteen

Detective Mitchell headed to the Pixard Theater in hopes of visiting Tyler Channing there. He was rather disappointed to find Tyler wasn't coming in on Sunday as part of his contract. He only reported for work on Sundays where there was a performance to be done, and since they had barely begun rehearsals, there was no need for him to not have a dedicated day off to spend with his family.

However, Caleb wanted to speak with the manager and some of the staff anyways, so he knew his visit wouldn't be totally wasted. He had to ask around, though, as to where the manager's office was located. One of the stagehands, paint on her cheek and nose, agreed to lead him to see Byron Cassiday, manager and producer for the current production. She knocked lightly on the door and opened it upon request from the husky voice inside.

"Mr. Cassiday? There's an officer here to see you."

"Really? Send him in, Jenny."

Jenny stepped back, holding the door open for the detective to proceed into the cramped office, shutting the door behind him before returning to work.

Byron stood up and stuck his hand out. "Hello, Officer. What can I help you with?"

Caleb shook his hand, then sat on the closest chair to him while Byron took his seat behind a paper-filled desk. He moved a couple of the stacks out of the way in order to see Caleb better.

"Actually, it's detective. I'm here to ask you about Louise Harper and Tyler Channing."

"Great. What did Louise do now? Or is this about the incident from a couple of days ago?"

"Why don't we start with the incident a couple of days ago?" Caleb pulled out his notepad in order to make notations while Byron talked.

"I've met Louise Harper a couple of times, but lately the woman is off her rocker. Do you know she came in here with baskets of muffins, fruit, gummy bears, and lord only knows what else just to see him? She won't leave the man alone. I think she can't distinguish the difference between the characters he's played and real life. I've heard of people like that, you know. Bothering actors, thinking they are the people they see on television or in the movies and that it's not just a role they play? I'd'a never thought Louise'd be that kinda person. Shows ya what I know, huh?"

Caleb remained stoic, just nodding in understanding. He learned long ago people will tell you a lot more than they mean to if left to their own verbal devices. "Go on," he encouraged.

"Well, Thursday, or was it Friday? No, Thursday, I see Mrs. Channing and her daughter come traipsing in, trying to find the dressing rooms. They'd brought Mr. Channing lunch from Kelli's Deli. Have ya ever eaten there? Food's dang good. We cater from them on opening and closing night. They're reasonable too. Not over-expensive, and their bread is always crispy, never soggy and never dry."

"Yes. I've been there. You were saying they were looking for the dressing rooms?"

"Yes. Yes. They were bringing Mr. Channing lunch. Since they weren't sure where his room was, I guided them. Although I didn't go in, standing back and all, I was close enough to hear the goings on when they entered his dressing room. Louise was in there. Mrs. Channing found Mr. Channing and Louise in an embrace, and boy did that tick off Mrs. Channing something fierce. I stood close by in case I was needed to physically break up them women."

"Did you hear anything they might've been talking about?"

"You kidding? They were loud enough to wake the dead. Louise was screaming that Tyler was hers. That she was with him first or they were together first. That shove come to shove, Mr. Channing was going to be with Louise. And Mrs. Channing was having a conniption fit about the whole thing, saying Mr. Channing was a no-good son of a bitch and she could have him. Then her and the kid stormed out. Tyler yelled at Louise to leave him and his family alone. That he'd never want her and if she didn't stay away, he'd kill her. Then he stormed out. I got a call from his P.A., Maggie, who said he won't come back to the theater unless there was better security. So I hired Guardian Security Services and are paying them 24/7 to be here and make sure Louise don't come sneaking in. She scares him off, and I'm going to lose a lot of money."

"How so?"

"Well, advertising, the security service, all his special needs with water and such. He ain't cheap, but a name like him in this production and I can charge three times the ticket costs. Maybe even four. But if Louise continues to screw it up, causing Mr. Channing and his family so much grief they leave, I'll be out of a shitload of money." He snorted. "Might want to kill her myself if she does that."

"Really?" Caleb jotted down some notes about Byron's comment. "Mind telling me where you were last night about nine?"

Byron tapped his chin in thought. "Here. I was having a staff meeting with Ms. Marian on wardrobe. We were here from about 8:30 until ten. I remember 'cause I was going to miss the ten o'clock news and I like the news. Why?"

Caleb jotted down a couple more notes, then put his pad away. He wanted his full attention on Byron in order to judge his reaction. "Louise Harper was murdered last night at about that time. If Ms. Marian confirms your story, then you'll both have an alibi."

"Murdered? I thought she was under arrest again for harassing the Channing family or some such. Murdered? I didn't do it. I got an alibi. Wait, you don't think Tyler did it? That'd ruin me for sure if he is accused of killing her."

"I'll need to talk to him first, before I can determine who the murderer is. I'd appreciate you keeping this news to yourself until tomorrow. I'd like to conduct my interviews without others knowing right away, if possible."

"Yeah. Yeah. Sure. Sure."

"Thank you." Caleb stood. "Is Ms. Marian, by any chance, here?"

"Yeah. She should be in the wardrobe locker. Just down the hall to the left. Third door on the right. You'll see the sign. If I were you, I'd ask her about the Channings and Louise. Her niece, Maggie, works for Tyler."

"Thank you."

Byron nodded, sitting back as he tried to comprehend the fact that Louise was now deceased.

Chapter Seventeen

Caleb couldn't miss the door to wardrobe even if he tried. The sign was huge and brightly colored. The door was slightly ajar, so he didn't bother knocking as he entered. The area was massive, yet there barely seemed to be much room to move around as it was crowded with rows and rows of costumes. If Caleb had to guess, he'd assume all one-hundred years of the theater's existence were displayed in costumes in this room.

Rather surprised he didn't see people bustling about, Caleb headed towards the one sound he could hear as soon as he entered. It was like walking in a maze. For one brief moment, Caleb felt like a mouse looking for the cheese in some colossal labyrinth. After a few moments of twists and turns around the racks of costumes, he found the source of the metallic clatter he'd heard the moment he pushed his way past the door.

A small, elderly woman, short gray hair and glasses on the bridge of her nose, hadn't realized she was no longer alone while she concentrated on the hem of a pair of khaki slacks. Caleb stood in the shadow watching her for a moment. She looked sweet and kindly, able to pass for anyone's grandmother. He was reminded of his own grandma, almost always seeming to have fresh-baked cookies from the oven for him whenever he visited.

Stepping forward, he cleared his throat to catch her attention. She looked up and frowned. "Sorry. No one is allowed back here."

"Mr. Cassiday told me where to find you. You are Ms. Marian?"

She nodded, still skeptical but a bit more welcoming. "Yes."

Caleb stepped forward, pulling out his badge. "I'm Detective Mitchell. I wanted to ask you some questions, if you don't mind."

She peered at the badge with her glasses, then pushed them farther up her nose and waved at a chair covered with outfits. "Push those aside and have a seat, young man. What kind of information can I help you with?"

Caleb moved the clothes and took a seat on the folding chair. Pulling out his notepad and pen, he flipped a couple of pages before he began. "I was wondering where you were last night?"

"I was with Mr. Cassaday. We had notes from Mrs. Falcon on what the actors should be wearing, but since it's a contemporary piece, a lot was left to our discretion. Mr. Channing had made a couple of recommendations on what he thought his character should wear specifically, and Mr. Cassiday and I were discussing them."

"What time would you say that occurred?"

"Well, now. Let me think. I guess we started about 8:15 or so. I have a pinochle group that meets on Fridays for dinner and a couple of hands. We're usually done about eight. I'd say we were here until about ten or 10:30. May I ask why?"

"Just checking. I'm also told you are the aunt to Maggie Keeler, the personal assistant to Mr. Channing?"

Her whole face seemed to light up with pride.

"Yes. She's my niece." Marian then frowned. "Is she in trouble?"

"Not that I'm aware. What can you tell me about her relationship to the Channings?"

"Oh, she likes her job and they seem to like her, though why they wouldn't, is beyond me. She's very organized and capable in her position."

"I'm sure she is. Does she tell you how they are all liking Valley View?"

"Oh my, yes. We talk at least once a week and, since she's been in town, even more so. She's very upset for Mr. Channing and having to deal with Mrs. Harper. I'm sure you know about the issues Mrs. Harper has created with Mr. Channing."

"Yes. I'm aware of a few things." He didn't want to give too much away. Not yet.

"Well, my dear Mags tells me a few things that I wouldn't normally repeat, but seeing as you're an officer of the law, I suppose it's okay to repeat them to you."

"Like what kind of things?"

"Well, Mrs. Harper has caused some old issues

to surface and it's put a strain on Mr. and Mrs. Channing."

"What kind of issues?"

"Seems Mr. Channing had an affair a couple of years ago and Mrs. Channing was ready to file for divorce. They agreed to see a marriage counselor instead to work on bringing the trust back into the marriage. They've been working on it steadily since. But Mrs. Harper has been telling Mrs. Channing that her and Mr. Channing have been together. Although, in the past. With the distrust Mrs. Channing already feels, Mrs. Harper's insinuations have just caused a rift between Mr. and Mrs. Channing. And their poor daughter has been caught in the middle. I'm sure Ms. Channing will be thrilled to start college in the fall and get away from her crazy parents."

"Do you know who Mr. Channing had the infidelity with two years ago?"

Marian pursed her lips in thought. "I'm sorry. I just don't remember that far back, but in all honestly, I don't remember what I had for breakfast either."

"It's okay. I'll check later to get the details." Caleb jotted in his notepad. "Have you seen Mrs. Harper here in the theater?"

"Yes. She was here a couple of days ago. Caused a bit of a ruckus when Mrs. Channing found them in his dressing room. Their yelling could be heard all over the theater. Mrs. Channing yelling if Mr. Channing and Mrs. Harper weren't anything then why were they embracing? Mr. Channing said he wasn't holding her in an intimate way but preventing her from leaving to spread lies about him. I just don't understand why Mrs. Harper won't leave that poor family alone. Did she do something else? Is that why you're here?"

"Sort of. Do you know if anyone wished harm to Mrs. Harper?"

"Other than Mr. or Mrs. Channing, no."

"The Channings wanted to hurt Mrs. Harper?"

"That fight the other day didn't make her very popular with either of them. I think they both wished she was dead to avoid the heartaches she was causing."

"Dead, huh?"

Marian waved her hand in a not-important sort of way. "Everyone says they wish someone was dead at one point or other. It's just a saying. Why?"

"Because Mrs. Harper was found murdered this morning."

"What? Murdered? Oh, that poor woman! You think Mr. or Mrs. Channing had something to do with it?"

"Possibly. You said yourself, Mrs. Harper was causing a lot of problems for both of them."

"True, but killing her wouldn't have solved them."

"Why not?"

"I just don't see those people stooping down to killing someone. They have too much to lose."

"I hope you're right." Caleb stood and tucked his notepad and pen in his upper breast pocket. "Thank you for your time." He handed her a business card. "Here's my number in case anything else comes to mind you want to tell me."

She took the card gingerly and set it on the table beside her. "I will."

Chapter Eighteen

Next stop was the Pennington Hotel. Caleb got out of his car, checking with the station as he did so for any update they might've had. He knew it was way too early for any labs to be back, those took at least 24 hours. More if they were backed up. The news had not yet been released either, so he didn't expect any tips. However, Davies or Simon might have uncovered more clues at the crime scene. He doubted it, as he was pretty thorough, but one never knew for sure.

If truth be told, however, he was hoping for a message from Mackenzie Harper. He knew she was still a suspect, but ever since he laid eyes upon her at Kendall and Skye's wedding, he couldn't stop thinking about her. Caleb also knew he had to focus on the case and not let his personal infatuation get the better of him.

With no messages, he entered the Historic Pennington and proceeded to the front desk. Showing his badge, he asked what room the

Channing's were in. He had to wait for the manager to be called forward to give his permission to let the Detective know what room due to privacy of their clients.

Getting off the elevator, knocking on the penthouse suite doo, a middle-aged woman with her turquoise hair pulled back in a bun answered. "May I help you?"

Caleb flashed his badge. "Detective Mitchell. May I come in?"

She looked at the badge closely. One couldn't be too careful. Stepping back, she opened the door wider. "Sure. Come on in. I assume this is about Louise Harper and the Order of Protection we filed?"

"We?" Caleb moved inside.

"I started the process on behalf of Tyler. Please sit." Maggie pointed to a chair at the dining room table. "Can I get you some coffee or water?"

"No thank you. I assume you're the personal assistant to Tyler Channing?"

"Yes sir. Maggie Keeler."

Caleb pulled out his notepad and pen, taking a moment to flip it open to a page he was looking for. "Why don't you tell me some of the issues you've had with Mrs. Harper?"

She chuckled. "Where do I begin? About a week ago, Tyler arrived. Debra, his wife and Pearl, his daughter, as well as I had been here two days prior preparing for his arrival. He had a meeting with his agent in New York before he could come here, so the ladies and I decided to come ahead of time."

"Is this a standard practice?"

"Not really, but he had to take the meeting in person, which is not unusual. Most agents prefer face to face meetings when possible. They feel it's more personal than phone or email."

"I see. Go on."

"Well, as I was saying, Tyler arrived last Sunday. A basket of gummy bears, fruit and Pringles had arrived."

"That's an odd gift basket."

"Those are his favorite things. Especially the

gummy bears."

"Ah. Makes sense then. Was there a note?"

"Yes. It was from Louise Harper. This was the first time any of us had heard of her, except Tyler, who stated he'd just met her in the elevator. He was a little flustered with the note and crumpled it almost immediately upon reading it. After they left, I admit I was nosey enough to dig through the trash and read it before throwing it away permanently."

"Do you remember what it said?"

"I doubt I'd ever forget. Please remember though, I am paraphrasing some of it. She basically said how wonderful it was to have him back in Valley View and it had been a long time since she's seen him. She also said she hoped they could pick up their love affair where they left off and she looked forward to…" Maggie blushed and looked away. "It got a bit graphic from there. Tyler was smart not to let Debra see it."

"Tyler and Debra have had issues in the past?"

Maggie still looked away, finally deciding on getting up to pour a glass of water from one of the bottles in the mini-fridge. "Sadly, yes. About two years ago. Debra caught Tyler cheating on her with his personal assistant back then."

"Debra isn't worried about that with you?"

Maggie laughed. "No. If anything, they'd worry about me with Debra. Or Pearl. But, I cherish my job a bit too much to mix my personal stuff with business. This is a great job and it pays very well. I wouldn't do anything to mess it up." She returned to her seat with the glass of water.

Caleb quirked a smile. "I see. So Louise left a very steamy note and met Tyler in the elevator upon his arrival?"

"Yes."

"I'm surprised Tyler and Debra are together after his previous infidelity, but I can understand why it was important to keep the information of Louise's note away from Debra."

"They'd almost gotten a divorce as a result of his last affair. Tyler didn't want to lose her though. She's the daughter of a big producer who almost exclusively uses him in his big productions. If they divorced, Tyler would lose a lot of work. Besides, I think he truly loves her."

"How did he get Debra to continue their marriage?"

"A lot of begging, pleading and offering to go to a marriage counselor in order to work on their problems and make their relationship stronger."

"Marriage counselor?"

"Yes. Dr. Grant Knox. He holds sessions as a conference call if they are not able to physically come in, otherwise he will see them at his office in San Bernardino. I think they planned on another call soon due to Louise. Although Debra didn't know about the first note, Tyler did tell her who the basket was from, stating she was just an ardent admirer. None of us knew what a crazy person she was."

"How so?"

"Well, most of it, I kept away from the Channing's. It's part of my job to handle the appointments, emails, snail mail responses, phone calls and general needs. Sunday night, Louise had caused such a problem for Tyler and Debra, they actually had her arrested. From what I understand, Louise showed up at the restaurant and caused a scene. She told Debra that Tyler was going to leave his wife for her. That Louise would be the one to make him happy. That she'd been with Tyler before Debra came into the picture and therefore he belonged to her. Louise did this all in front of a restaurant of people, including the mayor and his family, whom the Channing's were having dinner with.

We thought that would be the end of it, Louise being arrested and Tyler insisting she leave them alone. I later learned, earlier Louise had seen Tyler in his dressing room at the theater, so by the time the incident happened after dinner, he was beyond annoyed with her and her stunts."

"Was this the only day in which she bothered him?"

"Lord, I wish. Sadly, no. I kept a lot of it away from all three of them, but they might've found out another way. Hell, Louise might've told'em just to gloat. It seems once she got out of jail, she continued to try and talk or see him. I have what I call a stalker fan file." She pulled her computer over and reactivated it from the sleep mode. She pulled up the file, highlighted those just from Louise, transferred them to a new folder and turned the computer around for him to see the screen. "Here. You can see for yourself."

"Holy shit!" he couldn't help himself. There were 220 emails in the past week. Each one had a different heading. The first ones started out nicely, like hello, miss you, great to see you. Then they started to turn to headings like why don't you answer me? Or where are you? To becoming more insistent such as answer me now, or you'll regret not talking to me. He randomly picked a couple to open and skim. Some of the first ones had short messages, a couple in the middle talk about intimate acts, those near the end threatened about exposing him or worse, killing Debra unless he acknowledged her and wanted to be with her.

"I know. Tyler gets a few every now and again

of some super fan who can't separate real life from what they see on the screen. I've got tons of those, both email and snail mail that I just keep from Tyler and his family. Rarely this bad though. I mean, that's all in one week. Plus, she kept trying to see him. We caught her a couple of times trying to sneak in the hotel and Debra even spotted her a few days ago with a camera following them all over town. Debra was so angry, she snatched the camera, destroyed the SD card and busted the lens. Normally, I feel bad when that happens, but Louise had no respect for their privacy. I assume that's why you're here. About the camera? Is she going to sue? Debra was so furious when she came in, she didn't seem to care if they were sued or not for the camera. To her, it was worth it just to prove that Louise wasn't as sneaky as she thought she was." Maggie giggled slightly. "I would've given anything to see Louise's face when Debra confronted her. I heard she was pretty shocked."

"No. I'm not here for the camera incident." Although Caleb jotted down the details of the event.

"Where was everyone last night?"

"Last night? Don't tell me Louise is claiming we were with her?" Maggie shook her head. "The nerve of some people. You should see all the baskets and gifts she left about for Tyler. I got most of them before he even knew, but sheesh. Lace bra and panties set. A sex toy kit. Cattails. Handcuffs. Gummies up the wazoo. Unfortunately, some of the gifts arrived while Debra and Pearl were here. It really upset Debra to no end. They had worked so hard to get their marriage back on track so seeing Louise unravel it so easily was disheartening."

"Do you still have any of it?"

"Yes, along with the notes so I knew they were from her. I have them in my hotel room across the hall."

"May I have them for the investigation? As well as a copy of all these emails? And anything else you might have that belong to her?"

"Hell yes. You can have it all. Let me make a copy of those emails for you. Do you want them on a CD or just emailed to your box?"

"I'd prefer a CD if it's not too much trouble."

"No trouble at all." Maggie pulled the computer back around and dug in a nearby computer bag. "You asked about last night. Tyler was gone most of the evening. Debra and he got into another argument over Louise and he'd just had enough. He even thought about quitting the play and leaving Valley View just to get away from her, but then doubted at this point that she wouldn't just follow him wherever he went. Honestly, I think her veracity was beginning to disturb him greatly, especially after all the hard work he put in to get Debra to trust him again.

And Debra was rapidly losing trust that he hadn't done something with Louise to make her so neurotic. Tyler doesn't know I know, but she even kicked him out of bed on Thursday night and he's been sleeping on the couch ever since. Louise Harper has no idea what damage she is doing to this family."

"What time would you say Tyler got back to his room?"

"Well, let me think. Probably about 12:30 or 1am. I'm not entirely sure. I just know it was late."

"Where were you last night?"

"I had dinner with some relatives, then came back here about 9 to work on answering some emails and fan mail, doing inventory on stock autographed pictures to send."

"And Debra? Pearl? Were they here all night?"

"No. From what I understand, Debra and Pearl were going back to the Pixard Theater. They hoped to find Tyler and head out for a late dinner. I'm not sure what happened, but they all came back separately."

"What time would you say the ladies returned to the room?"

"Pearl was in about 11pm and I remember she was starting to get worried about Debra not being back yet then Debra showed up about 11:30, 11:40."

"But other than the Pixard, you don't know where either of them were all night?"

"As I said, I was with some family having

dinner, and I didn't feel it my business to know where they were. When they returned, they went into Pearl's room and shut the door so I couldn't overhear their conversation."

"And where is the family now?" Caleb closed his notebook putting the book and his pen in his upper breast pocket and stood. "I'd like to speak with each of them."

"They all went out to breakfast at The View Diner. They should be back any time soon. Can I ask what all of this is about? I'd rather not have the family disturbed over some silly nonsense Louise is trying to stir up."

"I guarantee that is not why I need to speak with them."

"Cryptic much? Never mind. You're welcome to stay until they return."

"I appreciate your offer, but can you send them all to the police station as soon as possible. I'll speak to them there."

"Sure. I'll let them know." Maggie moved to the door, holding it open for the detective to depart.

"They're not in any trouble, are they?"

"I'm afraid at this time, I can't answer that. Thank you for your time Ms. Keeler."

Chapter Nineteen

The Channing family walked into the police department. Tyler came in angry, upset that his day with his family was disturbed over some ludicrous reason having to do with Louise Harper. The woman had become an albatross as far as he was concerned. The fact she was wasting his time on a daily basis was becoming tiresome and redundant.

Debra didn't look any happier than Tyler did. She stormed right up to the desk, demanding the clerk's attention. "Detective Mitchell asked to see us. Tell him we're here but we have better things to do than to hang around a police station all day."

"And you are?" Sally knew who they were, but she'd be damned if she wouldn't make them wait by taking her time with the information before she called the Detective on his extension to inform him the Channing's were in the lobby.

"Who are we? What do you mean who are we? *THIS* is Tyler Channing. I'm his wife, Debra and the daughter of movie producer Harvey Maller."

"Okay. And your daughter's name?" Sally kept a straight face as she could see Debra getting more and more upset.

"Pearl Channing. Is this going to take much longer?"

Sally shook her head at the tone Debra was using. She could sympathize with the woman, to a point. After all, who wants to spend a beautiful Sunday afternoon inside of a police station. However, Sally would be more appreciative if Debra left the attitude at the door. Just because the woman was the daughter of, as well as married to a famous person, didn't mean the rest of the world was going to bow at her feet every second of every day. Not that Tyler Channing was any better. He was pacing, throwing angry looks every time he passed by. Sally would've made the call faster if they'd been a little less obnoxious. After all, like her mother always told her, you catch far more flies with honey that you do with vinegar. Sally moved slowly, asking for them to spell out each of their names, their address, phone and finally asking for their I.D.'s. She was sure they were going to have a spasm when she asked for the last few items. She didn't really need any of it since the detective was expecting them, but then Sally was also very detail oriented. Better to have it than have the detective wait while she got the information later on.

Finally, she had them take a seat before she called down to the detective's lair. Within minutes, Caleb came up and greeted the aggravated family.

Tyler was in his face immediately. "What's this all about? All Mags would say is that it has something to do with that bitch stalker, Louise. We have better things to do than to deal with that crazy nuisance."

Caleb gave him a polite smile. "All in due time, Mr. Channing. Actually, I'd like to speak to your daughter Pearl, first."

Debra jumped up and stood next to Tyler. The two had their arms folded almost making a wall to protect Pearl behind their human stance. Pearl came up behind them, laying a gentle hand on Debra's shoulder and Tyler's arm. "It's okay. I'd rather go first and get this over with."

Tyler put his arm around his daughter. "You ask for a lawyer if you start to feel uncomfortable of anything."

"I will. I promise." Pearl gave her father a small smile.

"I'm sure it won't come to that. I just need to get some general information. We won't be long at all." Caleb held the door open, ignoring the glare of Debra who refused to move one iota. Caleb smiled at her, a rarity for him in general. "Don't worry, Mrs. Channing. I'll be back for you shortly."

Pearl gave a small, nervous giggle as she passed through the door, letting Caleb shut it behind her, then direct her to which interrogation room they'd be using. He made sure the recording session sign was up and the equipment room was ready to start their session. Caleb then shut the door as he took a seat opposite of her.

"Thank you for being so willing to speak to me first."

"Anything to get away from the two of them.

Ever since Mags told them they had to come to the police station, they've made me miserable."

"I promise not to keep you too long. I just wanted to know where you were last night."

Pearl's eyes darted around the room, finally noticing the camera in the upper corner behind the detective. She looked at Caleb once, then her eyes roamed the room again as she shrugged her shoulders. She turned back to stare at him again.

"Mom and I went to the Pixard to see Dad, but he wasn't there. We hung for a few minutes, then left."

"What time was that?"

"I guess about 6 or 6:30 and left about 7:15 or so. I really wasn't paying much attention."

"Then what did you do?"

"I thought this was about that woman?"

"It is. I just need to establish a timeline so we can have a better idea of what went down."

"Oh. Afterwards, Mom said she had a few things she needed to do, so I left and headed to the cinema."

"What did you see? Anything good?"

Again, she shrugged her shoulders. "I saw Aladdin. I love the animated version and I think Will Smith is absolutely hysterical."

"What time did the show start?"

Pearl crossed her legs and leaned back looking entirely bored. "Around 9."

"After the show, what did you do?"

"Headed back to the Pennington."

"What time did you get back?"

"About 11:15 or 11:30. Not absolutely sure."

"Do you mind if I have your cell phone number? Just in case I have more questions?"

"No. I guess that's okay. It's 424-555-6983."

"Thank you. Did you see Louise Harper yesterday?"

"No. Was she following us again?"

"Again?"

"She was following us the other day, taking pictures and stuff. Mom got pissed big time and when we got back to the hotel, snuck up on her, grabbed her camera and destroyed it. Mom said that woman was worse than the paparazzi, though you'd think by now she'd be used to people stalking us to take our pictures. We are in all the tabloids. What difference was it if the Harpy took pictures of us or not? But mom was pretty upset with her in general."

"Harpy?"

"Louise Harper. Harper. Harpy. Get it?"

"Ah, I see. And why was she pretty upset in general?"

Pearl tilted her head slightly. "Mom and dad have marriage issues. Grandpa wants mom to leave dad. Dad is fighting to stay together and regain mom's trust. They been dealing with problems for the last couple of years. Louise is bringing about a lot of those insecurities my mom has. It's making it hard for mom. *She's* making it hard on mom."

"I see. You didn't answer the original question. Did you see Louise yesterday?"

"Oh. Sorry about that. No."

Caleb felt she wasn't telling him the whole truth, but he didn't have proof at the moment, so he let it go for the time being. Eventually, he was sure he'd find out who she was protecting.

"I thank you for your time, Miss Channing. I'll see you back to the lobby." He stood and waited for her to follow suit returning her to where her parents were waiting.

"Mrs. Channing? May we speak?"

Debra and Tyler both looked up from their seats as the door opened, the former standing upon request and headed through the door Pearl emerged from.

Once they were both seated, Debra crossed her arms, taking an angry, defensive stance.

"Look. I'll save you some time. I admit it. I did it. I know I shouldn't have, but I was at the end of my rope. I mean, I'm used to being followed and I'm used to Tyler having ardent fans, but Louise was different. She kept finding us and making it a point that her and Tyler have been together. She thinks they should be together now. Pushing. She's always pushing. It's enough to dive anyone insane. Can't you see that? Can't you understand? I had to do it!"

Caleb's eyebrows raised. He'd heard confessions before, but none given so easily. Which made him wonder what exactly she was confessing to. "Excuse me? You did what?"

"I assumed you were talking to us because Louise complained about her camera. I admit it. I destroyed it. She's lucky though. I should've bashed it against her head and knocked some sense into her."

He pinched his nose for a moment, though he didn't confirm nor deny her assumption. "Thank you for admitting that. Can you tell me where you were last night?"

It was Debra's turn to appear taken aback. She wondered why he wanted to know since the camera episode was a couple of days ago. Was Louise accusing her of something other than the camera incident? "I was at the theater until sevenish."

"And after you left?"

"Pearl and I split up. She wanted to go to a movie, but I wasn't interested. Instead, I went to some small diner and sat for a few hours enjoying the peace and quiet."

"What's the name of the diner?"

Debra shrugged. "I didn't pay much attention."

"Where was it located?"

"I don't know this area super well. Near the theater I'd guess. I walked there."

"When do you and Pearl split up?"

"Almost as soon as we left the Pixard. We stood outside and talked about what we wanted to do, then went our separate ways. I wasn't ready to go back to the hotel. I'd no interest in the movie. To be truthful, that Harper bitch has just caused so many issues between me and my husband, I needed time to think and decide if I wanted to stay on by continuing to fight or just let her have him."

"Was that even a choice?" For the first time since Caleb had seen Debra, she unfurled her arms. Conspiratorially she leaned forward. "Yes. You see, Ty and I have been having issues the past couple of years."

"He cheated on you?"

"Pearl must've told you. Or Maggie did. Either

way, it doesn't matter. I know the tabloids suspect we're having trouble. I'm having a hard time trusting him. We're even seeing a shrink to try and help, but lately, the littlest thing sets me off. He's an actor and a damned good one. How do I tell if he's acting or being truthful? And I just wonder if it's all worth fighting for anymore. You know what I mean?"

This was so not his area of expertise. Normally, getting involved in personal relationships made him uncomfortable. However, Mackenzie Harper occupied his every thought. They hadn't even been out on an official date, but he felt he 'd hate to have something happen that would prevent him from trusting her in any way. Or her trust him. For once in his life, he could sympathize with what Debra must be going through. What she was feeling.

"How long have you two been together?"

"I met him about twenty-one years ago. We've been married for nineteen. I'd gotten pregnant with Pearl just a couple of months before we got married, but we'd planned a wedding before I got pregnant."

Caleb nodded in nonjudgmental understanding. "When did you return to your hotel?"

Debra once again leaned back and crossed her arms. It was a physical indication she was trying to distance herself once again, even if she wasn't aware she was doing it. "About midnight I guess. I wasn't really paying attention. I didn't think I'd need to account for my whereabouts for any reason."

"Was everyone else at the hotel when you got there?"

She tilted her head in thought for a moment, then shrugged. "I think so. I don't remember seeing Tyler, but then I've had him sleeping on the couch the last couple of nights. Maggie was working on fan mail. I remember that and Pearl was waiting for me when I got in. She was upset, so I went to her room and we talked for a bit."

"Upset about what?"

"I'm not really sure. She wouldn't tell me, exactly, but she hasn't been too thrilled with the arguments Tyler and I have been having of late, so

I'm sure it was just a further manifestation of our marital concerns."

"Is there some reason that she's so worried about you two breaking up? I mean, I understand when young kids have to deal with their parents marital issues, but she's nineteen. I'm just a bit surprised to find it affecting her so."

Debra shrugged again. "You have to understand, Detective, we come from a land of the big screen and it's rare to see marriages last long in Hollywood. Tyler and I are a bit of a rarity, in some cases. Pearl had seen her friend's families broken and she's seen the toll it's taken on her friends. Nineteen is old enough to drive and vote, but is it really mature enough to handle the complexities of a bitter divorce? Is any age?"

"I admit, it's a bit different here in the Midwest. I apologize that I hadn't understood the pressure she might be going through. What time did you leave Pearl's room?"

"I guess it was about two in the morning when I headed to bed. I do remember trying to be quiet so not to wake Tyler who was snoring on the couch."

"Did you see Louise Harper at any time yesterday?"

"Thankfully, no. I'm to the point right now that if I saw her, I'm probably punch her in the nose just for all the aggravation she's caused."

"Alright Mrs. Channing. I don't think I have anything else to ask right now. I'll bring you back to the lobby where you can wait while I speak to Mr. Channing."

"Why do you need to speak to him? I already told you I did it. Tell me how much I owe her, and I'll write a check right now to cover the cost of a new camera."

Caleb stood. "Sadly, Mrs. Channing, this isn't about the camera or the pictures she took of you. It's about someone viciously attacking and killing Louise last night."

After a perceptible pause, Debra stood up. "Somehow, I'm not surprised, but I didn't do that."

Chapter Twenty

Tyler got into the interrogation room, but instead of sitting down, he leaned over the table threateningly. "I want to know what this is all about. You've wasted my time and my family's time over some idiotic woman who can't tell the difference between real life and make believe and who won't leave me and my family alone. Whatever you said has my wife upset when you brought her back and I don't appreciate that either. And over what? A broken camera? Getting her arrested? Trying to avoid her and keep her away from us? This is bullshit. Arrest her and leave us alone. Whatever she is accusing us of, I'm sure she's lied about it."

"She didn't lie about this, Mr. Channing. Trust me. Why don't you sit down so we can talk?"

"No. Either tell me what this is about, arrest me or I'm leaving."

Caleb sat down, ignoring the fact Tyler was now hovering over him as he leaned on the opposite end of the table. The intimidation tactic wouldn't work on the detective. "Mr. Channing. Either sit and talk to me, or I will have you arrested, and we will talk with you in cuffs instead. Either way, we are going to have this conversation."

Tyler hesitated a few more moments, but he realized the detective wasn't fooling around. "Fine." He pulled out the chair and plopped it in, folding his arms over his broad chest.

"Okay. Let's get started." Caleb opened his notepad up. "Did you see Louise yesterday?"

"No."

"Did you talk to Louise yesterday?"

"No."

"What did you do yesterday?"

"Met with Guardian Security Company to go over the specifics of protection while I was working at the theater."

"What time did you leave their offices?"

"Five."

"Then where did you go?"

"I headed back to the theater."

"Pearl and Debra said they went to the theater to find you about 6:30. You weren't there. Where were you?"

"I left the theater about 6:15. I must've just missed them."

"Where did you go then?"

"What's this all about?

"Please just answer the questions."

Tyler gave a small growl in aggravation. "Grabbed a bite to eat."

"And last night?"

"I'm sure your aware, Debra and I are having a few issues. I went to the train yard to let her cool off."

"Why the train yard?"

"I've always been intrigued by trains since I was a kid. Watching them relaxes me. And I didn't think Louise would be able to find me there."

"What time did you leave?"

"It was late."

"What time?"

"I guess it was about one in the morning. When

are you going to tell me what Louise has accused me of."

Caleb took a deep breath as he leaned forward. "Mrs. Harper hasn't accused you of anything. She hasn't accused anyone of anything. She was murdered last night, and we are trying to figure out who did it."

Tyler's mouth dropped open. "She was *what?* You mean, she's dead?"

That's what murdered means. Dead. Caleb thought. "Yes. That's what I mean."

"How? Do you think *I* did it? Of course you do. That's why all the questions. Needing to obtain my alibi." A thin line of sweat beaded along the crest of his hairline, which didn't go unnoticed by the detective.

A knock on the door caused Caleb to stand. "Excuse me." He headed just outside where Davies was waiting for him with a small folder in hand. "We got some of the prints back, but they don't match anyone in the system."

Caleb scanned the folder contents quickly.

"Why don't you offer the Channing family some refreshments? They've been here a while. Start with some water for Tyler."

Davies nodded and headed to get some glasses and water. He knew exactly what Caleb was asking him to do and he had no problems being underhanded to figure out who killed someone so gruesomely.

Caleb waited a couple of moments before he headed back in, with the folder in hand. He'd just sat down again, across from Caleb when Davies knocked on the door bringing in two glasses of water. He carefully touched them in such a way as to not interfere with their fingerprints when they lifted the cup to drink it. Then the officer quietly headed out of the room again. Caleb knew he was going to also bring in a couple of cups of water to the two Channing women in the lobby. Once they threw their cups away, or left them behind, the cups would then be considered trash and therefore the police could confiscate them without needing a warrant to have them tested for both fingerprints and DNA.

Caleb reached out and took a sip from the cup Davies gave him. "Sorry about that. So, you said you didn't see Louise at all yesterday?"

Tyler squirmed. "Yeah." He was getting hot and downed the water in just a couple off gulps.

"Would you like some more?"

"Depends. How long are you going to keep me?"

"Depends on how truthful you are with me."

"What do you mean?"

"I mean you're awfully nervous for someone who isn't involved."

"I'm just nervous in general, Detective. It's not like one gets to be a real suspect in a murder of someone you only wish was dead. However, just because I wished it doesn't mean I did it. People wish others dead all the time but they don't act on it. I didn't kill her. I just wished she'd leave me and my family alone." Tyler knew he was rambling, but the whole proceedings had him discombobulated.

"And if she didn't? Would you have forced the

issue by making sure she never bothered any of you again?"

"No. If she didn't leave us alone, I'd've had her arrested for violating the order of protection. That's your job to handle stuff like that. Not mine. I'd've gladly let you deal with putting her away permanently. I do have a reputation to protect and murdering some overzealous, mentally challenged woman isn't going to protect that reputation. I'd rather be the martyr than the aggressor."

"Would you mind rolling up your sleeves?"

Tyler was perplexed. "Why?"

"I found part of a picture and the man in the photo had a tattoo on his forearm. Do you have any tattoos?"

"I used to. I had a tattoo of cannabis leaves on my forearm, but I had it removed decades ago. With a new family, it didn't seem appropriate. A stupid, youthful indiscretion that didn't suit my adult life, family or career."

"Okay Mr. Channing. I'd ask that you and your family don't leave town. We may have more questions for you later."

Caleb stood up, opening the door for Tyler to proceed him back to the lobby. He gave Davies a nod who went into the interrogation room to collect the cup used by Tyler as evidence and send it to the lab. He led the family out to the front, where he watched as they returned to the parking lot and their rental car. Behind him, Davies was also collecting the women's cups. No stone unturned, everyone gets checked. Caleb watched the family as they climbed into the car and left, wondering which one was holding the biggest secret.

He thought about pulling out his phone to call Mackenzie, but he realized he had nothing new to tell her and just wanting to hear her voice was no reason to get in contact with her. There was a part of him that hated his own morality. He just couldn't date a suspect, even if he was sure she was innocent. It'd be a conflict of interests once it went to court and he wouldn't dare risk having the case thrown out due to a technicality involving his desires. He clenched his fists a couple of times to get back under control before returning inside to continue working on the case.

Chapter Twenty-One

The worse thing about detective work was waiting on lab results and phone records, both of which he'd submitted for yesterday. He'd turned in several requests for print comparison to those found at the bloody scene. He'd made sure he had gotten the Channing's, but earlier he'd also managed to get Mackenzie's, Al's and Maggie's as well as a few in the theater. Thank goodness for the beat cops able to do all the strenuous legwork involved in a case like this. The officer's also got each of their DNA samples, but those took longer. He'd visited a judge late in the afternoon and obtained warrants for the phone records of each of those involved in the case and had the officers check on the alibis of all the suspects. The more he could eliminate, the more he could focus on the likeliest killer. Caleb could only hope some results would be in sooner rather than later.

He almost felt like his hands were tied while he waited. However, there was still a ton of evidence to go through taken from the house. Pulling on a pair of gloves, he opened the first box and began to rummage through it, looking for anything that would give him some idea of who the perpetrator was.

The house had been ransacked and part of him wondered if they found whatever they had been looking for. If they did, would there be enough evidence left behind that Caleb could figure out what it entailed? He could only hope.

One of the things recovered from the home were some charred papers in the fireplace. Pulling out a plastic bag, he hoped he'd be able to recover enough to determine what they were in reference to and put him in the right direction in order to find what Louise may have been killed for, although he was still under the suspicion that her murder was not planned but more of an impetuous action. After all, there were two empty wine glasses as well as some cheese and crackers. Who'd go through all of that trouble if the intent was murder. No, this was more of a social meeting that turned vicious.

Sifting through the ashes of the paper remains, most were indiscernible. Caleb was able to find a couple of remnants with the names Lucas and Lily. At first he wondered who they were, and it filled him with glee realizing he'd have to ask Mackenzie about them. Although she was part of the investigation, and professionally, he had to keep his distance, this provided him an opportunity to see her. Sure, he could call her and get the info over the phone, but he wanted to see her, and any excuse would do. At least he now had a legitimate reason to contact her if only to find out for sure who Lucas and Lily were? What did they have to do with Louise? Was one of them her guest? Did one of them kill her and try to hide their involvement by burning the papers? Each clue only led to more questions. He rummaged through the soot and ash only to find another remnant. This one looked like a Facebook post with a very intimate scene occurring between the two. Then something clicked. He pulled out his notepad and rummaged through the interviews he had taken. Yep, there it was. On his talk with Mackenzie, she mentioned her mother was addicted to role play on Facebook. It stood to reason that Lily might be the character Louise portrayed in that game. And Lucas? From Mackenzie's interview, he knew that was Louise's play partner. He realized Louise's obsession with Tyler was the avatar her partner was using, which could also account for her addiction to the real Tyler Channing. But, who did Louise play against? Who was the real person behind the persona of Lucas. He'd have to ask the tech department to trace the IP address to see if they were involved in any way.

Jotting down a couple of questions he wanted to make sure he didn't forget, Caleb continued sifting through the papers found in Louise's home. Most of the information was with regards to her bank statements, and housing payments. Taxes and insurances. Nothing that would give him further information as to who killed her.

He realized he was getting stiff hunched over all the papers. Standing he stretched, when the phone rang. "Detective Mitchell."

"Hello detective. This is county calling. I have some preliminary results of your fingerprints."

"Perfect. Did they come back to anyone in the system?"

"No. But we're still comparing them to those you sent us yesterday afternoon. That will take us another couple of hours."

"Great. What about the DNA results?"

"We're still working on those. They won't be back for at least 24 hours yet."

"Any news from tech over getting through the passwords on the computer? Or getting info on the IP address of Lucas?"

"I've not heard from tech, but that's another department. I'll give them a call to contact you with updates."

"I'd appreciate that. Keep me informed, please."

"10-4." Police slang for understood.

Hanging up the phone, Caleb dialed Mackenzie. He listened to it ring three times, then that sweet voice he'd longed to hear answered on the fourth.

"Hello?"

"Hello, Mackenzie. This is Detective Mitchell. I was wondering if I could buy you coffee at the Hungry Hamster. I have a few more questions to ask you about your mom's case."

"Of course, Detective. I'm free this afternoon, so whenever you'd like, just let me know."

"Caleb please. How about in an hour?" He wanted to freshen up and change his shirt which now had soot smudges on it.

"An hour would be perfect. I'll see you then." Mackenzie hung up; her stomach suddenly filled with a swarm of butterflies. Why was she so nervous? She was anxious to get her mother's killer brought to justice and her mother's stuff released so her father and her could start planning the funeral and getting her affairs in order. She'd had to remember to ask Caleb when all of that could occur, although she was very aware the coroner was still doing the autopsy and it would likely be at least a couple of days. Maybe she could talk Caleb into letting her into her mother's house so she could at least get some of the paperwork for the insurances. She knew her dad was anxious to get into the house as well. It was, after all, his home. He'd only moved out as a result of their marital separation.

According to him, Louise forced him to go. She was tired of having him around and dealing with him.

"Al is married to his work, not to me. He doesn't seem to care whether I'm around unless it's to pick up after him or make his dinner. He can hire a maid for that." Louise told Mackenzie once during their Sunday morning breakfasts after church. "There is no intimacy. We are two strangers living in the same house. At best we are roommates and I don't need a roommate in my life."

"Why don't you do something to change it?" Mackenzie asked, sipping her coffee between bites of pancakes.

"I tried. I'd suggest we go out to dinner, or to the show. I offered to go to the ballgame or some other kind of date-like event. Sure, he'd go, but he never planned anything. And when he was home, it was either on his own computer or phone or sleeping. How is that a relationship with me? It's not. It's a relationship with the electronic world. Then he got me my own computer and I just fell into the same routine. At least on there, I found someone who cares about me. Who is interested in me and my day. Who asks to spend time with me. I don't have to always come up with plans to spend time with him. It's not forced."

"Him? Who?"

"His name is Lucas. Or, rather, that's the name he uses online."

"So he could be anybody?"

"Yes, and he knows me as Lily. It's all good. It's a game and those are our character's names. But we also talk in chat while we are playing. We talk about what we want in life and what we did during the day. He asks about you and work and all sorts of things. The conversation isn't forced."

"He's not real! God, mom. Don't you see, he could be anybody. A serial killer or a rapist. With the information you are telling him, how do you know he's not draining your social security or bank accounts."

Louise chuckled and patted Mackenzie's hand. "I don't give him that kind of information. I'm not stupid, Mackenzie. I just am tired of being alone with a man I'm supposed to be married to. Lucas cares about me. Al doesn't seem to know I even exist unless he needs clean underwear or dinner." Louise sighed. "I'm tired Mackenzie. Tired of working on a marriage that doesn't seem to go anywhere and staying with a man who doesn't care to be with me. I'm tired of being used as a maid and cook. We don't even hold hands, or sleep in the same room. Even when he's home and awake, he isn't there. He hasn't asked me to do anything in so long, I can't even remember the last time and I'm tired of always having to ask him to spend time with me. That's not the way a marriage should be. That's not the way *life* should be. There's more to a relationship than a house in both your names and a piece of paper that says you're married. There's more to just being together than sharing his last name." A lone teardrop fell from Louise's eye, and she quickly brushed it away.

Mackenzie moved closer to her mom and gave her a hug. "I'm sorry. I hadn't realized it had degraded so badly between you two."

"Don't get me wrong, Mackenzie. He has never hit me, abused me or called me names. But ignoring I exist is just as bad as any of the other things he could've done."

Shortly after that conversation, Al moved to an apartment nearby. Louise figured if she was alone, she might as well live alone. Al had thought it would only be temporary and he'd be back in a month or so, but it'd been eight months since she kicked him out. Mackenzie believes he never understood how he'd made his wife feel. Neglecting someone was just as bad as abusing them.

However, with Louise now deceased, there was no reason why he couldn't go back to the house he was still paying the mortgage for.

With less than an hour, Mackenzie brushed her

teeth and her hair and quickly choose a loosely fitted sundress with a pair of sandals. Thankfully, she'd gotten a pedicure just the other day, so she knew her feet looked cute. Grabbing her keys and phone, she dashed through the door. She'd probably be early to the Hungry Hamster, but that was okay. After all, Caleb wouldn't realize she was anxious to see him. It'd been a few days.

Along the drive, Mackenzie thought of something and used her hands-free device in her car to call Kendall. It barely rang once before Kendall answered.

"Hello, Mackenzie. How are things going? Are you doing okay?"

"Hey, Kendall. I'm doing okay. It's a bit frustrating not being able to prepare for mom's final wishes, but until they finish their investigation, there isn't anything we could do. How about you? How is married life treating you?"

Kendall laughed. "Tinkerbell is still getting used to the new house we bought just before our wedding. There are so many rooms for her to explore and she's not sure which she likes best. Plus, we've only been back for a week or so, and she's still upset we left her for our honeymoon."

Mackenzie laughed. "I can only imagine. Look, I won't keep you, but I was wondering if you talked to the police about mom's murder."

"No. I thought they would want to talk to me, but I've not heard from anyone."

"Hmm. I'm rather surprised. I'm on my way to see the detective on the case."

"Well, tell him I might have some information that'd be helpful. Although tonight, Skye and I are going to a retirement party for one of the firemen he works with. I'd rather not have to talk to the police tonight."

"I'll let him know that as well. Thanks Kendall."

Mackenzie disconnected just as she pulled into the Hungry Hamster's parking lot. Yep, she was early, but that was okay. She wondered what information Kendall might have that would help solve the case or if it was going to be of any interest at all. Regardless, Mackenzie checked her lipstick and hair, then ventured inside the restaurant.

Since it was midday on a Monday, the place was pretty empty. The sign at the hostess booth read to seat yourself, so she chose one that could be seen from the door and yet offered a bit of privacy from the other customers. She was nervous, shaking slightly, more butterflies fluttering around her belly and making her a bit nauseous.

"Hi. I'm Anne. What can I get you to drink?"

"Just a cup of herbal tea please. I'm waiting for someone else." Though why she added the latter bit, she was unsure. It wasn't like this was a date and they were going to share a meal together. Not that she could eat anyways.

As the waitress moved away, Caleb walked in and spotted her immediately. He strode over and she couldn't help noticing how good he looked in a pair of jeans and a polo.

"Hi. Thanks for meeting me."

"My pleasure. Any word on the case?"

"Not yet, but it takes time. I have a couple of

follow up questions for you. I thought it might be nicer to meet someplace other than the station or your place."

"Thank you for your thoughtfulness. I do appreciate not having to go to the police station if I don't have to."

Caleb had carried a folder in with him, so he opened up it. "Do you know a Lucas really is? Was your mother portraying Lily?"

Mackenzie paled. "Why do you ask?"

Caleb shifted into detective mode, becoming stoic so as not to give too much away. Her response was disconcerting. Usually one who had something to hide answered a question with a question. "I found the name among your mother's papers. It was paired with Lucas who you mentioned was the person your mother role played with. I'm assuming your mom was Lily, but I wondered if you knew who played Lucas."

Mackenzie shifted uncomfortably. Maybe she shouldn't have worn the dress as her now sweaty thighs were sticking to the vinyl seats. "Oh."

"Who are they?"

"You're correct. Mom was Lily. Lucas was the person she played that Facebook role playing game with, but I'm not sure who that person really was. It could be anyone, right? Though the Lucas character, as I mentioned before, used Tyler Channing's picture as his avatar."

"I thought that was what you'd said in our interview earlier, but I just wanted to clarify. You have no idea who was behind the facade of Lucas?"

"No. I'm not even sure if it was anyone here in town. They could've been some guy out in Yemen for all I know."

Anne brought Mackenzie her tea and asked the detective what he would like.

"Coffee, please." Caleb waited until the waitress left and returned with a cup of the hot, steamy black joe. He put in an individual container of cream and stirred it, all the while watching Mackenzie who, despite looking ravishing in a breezy sundress, looked very ill at ease.

Once they were alone again, Mackenzie spoke.

"When are my dad and I able to get into the house again. I know dad would like to move back in and not have to pay rent anymore and I'd like to get some of my mother's papers in order so we can prepare for her funeral and all."

"I can't let you back in the house for a while yet. We are still processing it. However, I can probably get you the papers you need. Just tell me what you are looking for and I'll see what I can do."

"Sure. Mostly, they are the insurance papers. They should be in the bottom right drawer of her desk. When do you think we will have the death certificates?"

"It'll take another couple of days for the autopsy to be completed. Once that is finished, we'll be able to let you all back into the house and give you the death certificates as well as her remains for whatever final arrangements you plan on making."

Mackenzie jumped when Caleb's phone rang.

"Excuse me. I need to take this." Caleb slid out of the booth and moved to a more remote location by the door so she couldn't leave while he was preoccupied.

Mackenzie became more nervous as he kept sending glances her way while on the phone. He nodded one final time and returned to the booth.

"Mackenzie Harper. I'm going to need you to stand and turn around."

She nervously followed his instructions. "Why?"

"You are under arrest for the murder of Louise Harper." He sadly admitted. It was just his luck the woman he was interested in personally was a murderer.

Caleb put her in cuffs, just as a patrol car pulled up. Officer Simon entered the building and headed right for them. "Take her to the station, Mark and read her, her rights. I'll be there shortly."

"Wait. You can't do this. I'm innocent. Why would I kill my mother? Please. Don't do this." Mackenzie called back as Officer Simon led her out and to the back of the squad.

Caleb pulled a five from his wallet and left it

on the table, then headed to his own car to drive back to the station, feeling sick the whole way.

After he got into his car, his phone rang. "Mitchell here."

"Hi. I'm Oliver with County Tech Department. I just wanted to let you know we finally got into Harper's computer and traced the IP address for the Lucas character. I'm sending over the file for your review."

"Can you give me a brief rundown of your findings?"

"Yeah. I think you'll be very surprised."

Caleb raised his eyebrows. "Anything more than that?"

"Not over the phone, sir. You'll see why when you read my report. You should have it within the next couple of hours. I don't want to take the chance anyone other than you sees the report by faxing it over."

"Alright. Thank you for letting me know." Disconnecting the handsfree device, Caleb mumbled to himself. "That was awfully cryptic."

However, it did give him a bit of hope to free Mackenzie, even if he did, at that moment, really believe she was the culprit.

Chapter Twenty-Two

Caleb entered the station and went to booking. Mackenzie had just been brought in ahead of him and was being printed and photographed. When she was completely processed, Mark brought her to the interrogation room where Caleb was waiting.

"I didn't kill my mother." She stated matter-of-factly as she sat down. Her eyes were rimmed red as was her nose, indicating she'd been crying. "Why would you think I had?"

"You lied to me. You said you hadn't seen your mother in a couple of days, but we found a bag with a receipt for the empty wine bottle in the garbage dated earlier that day. When we checked the store monitors, you were the one who purchased it. Which means you went over there after you bought it. Which also means you were probably the last to see her. We are checking your prints now to those found on the bottle and around the house."

Mackenzie seemed to deflate. "Yes. I bought the wine. I'd hope to talk to her about taking dad back and about the whole issue of her bothering the Channing Family. I wanted her to recant her statements that Tyler was my father, not Al. I felt she should know how hurtful it was to all of us if she continued to spread those lies. But, I swear, it was earlier in the evening though. About 8 when I was there. Look at the time stamp on the store video. After I bought the wine, I went right to her place and she lives only ten minutes from the store."

"That just makes it worse for you, Mackenzie. You could've been there for a couple of hours enjoying the wine before you stabbed her."

"But I wasn't. We didn't open the wine. Shortly after I got there, she was trying to tell me that Tyler was my father and show me some proof with pictures and stuff. I saw that picture you tried to show me yesterday. The man was Tyler Channing. She was using that as proof that she was with him before I was born. That he's my father and not Al. That she'd been hiding it all these years because she didn't want to burden Tyler with being a father and strapped with a family he didn't want because he was just beginning his career and she knew it was important to him."

"What time would you say you left then?"

"Only a couple of minutes later. We got into the fight almost immediately. Even took the verbal argument onto the front lawn. Ask her neighbors. I'm sure with as loud as we were, one of the neighbors noticed us. I was gone by 8:30 at the latest. Please. You have to believe me. I didn't agree with my mom, but I'd never want to see her dead, much less kill her."

She was going to hate him, but there was nothing he could do about it. Maybe, one day, she'd forgive him, if he could forgive himself for not believing in her. It wasn't that he didn't want to, he had just seen too much cruelty in the world to take words at face value, especially when Mackenzie had already lied to him. Why couldn't she have told him the truth right from the start? "I'm sorry, Mackenzie. Until I can verify everything, you'll have to stay in holding." Still, he wasn't ready to leave her to that fate yet. "Did she show you anything other than the picture?"

Mackenzie's cheeks turned bright red and she looked down at the table. "Yes. She showed me some of the scenes she had as Lily with Lucas. She told me that was proof Tyler knew it was her because he wouldn't be that passionate online with someone he didn't know intimately." She looked up at him, pools of water glistening in her hazel eyes. "Do you know what it's like to have your very existence in question? To not be sure who your father is? Where you come from? To think, even if you don't believe it deep down, but have the doubt placed there, that everything you knew was a lie? And then, to see those threads she'd printed? Of them doing things no daughter should have to think of her mother doing, even though in order to be alive, you know she did? It's unimaginable."

Caleb reached over and grabbed a couple of tissues on the table nearby, handing them to her. He totally comprehended the doubt one could have when a lie was brought into the mix. "I understand. It must have been hard for you to deal with that.

Which is why, in a fit of rage you plunged the corkscrew into her body, forcefully killing her. I know it was an accident and not something planned."

"It wasn't even that. Oh my god. Do you mean to tell me, that's what she was killed with? A corkscrew? We never even opened the wine. I was only there for a few minutes before we got into that heated argument. I swear. Ask the neighbors. They will tell you about the yelling and screaming we did on the front lawn before I got into my car and drove away. I'm telling you the truth." She blew her nose loudly, using another tissue to wipe her cheeks dry.

Caleb desperately wanted to believe her. But even if she was innocent, he doubted she'd be interested in having anything to do with him now. "I'll check it all out. I promise. If everything you said is true, I'll have you out as soon as feasibly possible. Right now, we have to lock you up while we investigate. I *am* sorry." He stood and left the room waving Officer Simon in to put her in a holding cell.

Needing a time to regroup, Caleb headed down to his closet-like office, shut the door and buried his head in his hands. He hadn't had a chance to even ask her for a date or really get to know her, so why was arresting her and putting her in jail so bothersome to him. He felt guilty. His instincts had rarely proven him wrong, but he admitted he had a huge attraction to this particular woman from the first moment he saw her at the wedding. Had he let his infatuation blind him to her true nature? Or was he feeling disturbed about locking her up because he knew she must be innocent? But all the evidence he had pointed to Mackenzie, albeit, not everything had come back from the labs yet and there was still the confirmation to attain from the neighbors of her alibi that she'd left the house in a ferocious rage. Only, he wasn't sure if that made it worse for her or not, since Louise was obviously murdered in the throes of anger. Mackenzie could've returned to the house and killed her mother. She already admitted they'd been involved in a heated argument. He was making himself crazy going back and forth, and he knew it wouldn't even be an issue if he wasn't infatuated with her.

A knock on the door and he quickly pulled himself together. "Enter."

"Sorry to disturb you, sir, but the autopsy was just sent over." Sally held the manila folder out to him.

"Thank you." He grabbed it from her and opened it to read the results of Louise's autopsy. Maybe something here would help save Mackenzie. He skimmed it quickly, then sat back and reread it with a fine-tooth comb, picking up and analyzing all the details contained within.

The first pages were the main records of name, date, age, height, weight, and cause of death signed by the doctor who performed the procedure. Cause of death: Multiple stabbing with a metal object containing a spiral appendage.

The next page had a mockup drawing of a body with mark ups as to where Louise had been stabbed. There were two major points, each numbered one and two consecutively. The first wound was her left eye. From the written report which accompanied it the notation, the wound was deep enough to just pierce her brain. The second blow to Louise probably wasn't necessary, but the suspect pushed the object into Louise's neck severing her carotid artery. If the first blow didn't kill her, the second surely did.

From the description of the weapon, length and shape of the object used for the stabbing, the corkscrew they'd found while searching the place was the most likely instrument of the assault. Turning the page, Caleb nodded silently as the doctor confirmed the corkscrew as being the weapon. What a hideous way to die, but was Mackenzie really the culprit?

In his gut, he really didn't think so, but then his judgement may be clouded with his personal feelings. He pulled out his computer and pulled up the recording of the interview. His heart ached at the hurt look in her eyes when she avoided the first round of questions until he probed her further with results of the store video, fingerprints on the wine bottle and witness statements that she was there when she said she wasn't. One only lies when they have something to hide and it seemed reasonable she was lying because she murdered her mother in a fit of rage. At least according to the evidence they had so far.

"Damn it." He muttered and focused on the interview. Mackenzie provided a few people he could talk to in order to prove her innocence. He jotted down the details and called in the officers assisting him on the investigation to go talk to the neighbors. He still had to follow up on the warrant for the phone records of the Channing Family, as well as Mackenzie, Al and some of the theater staff. As such, Caleb hoped between the officers and his own deductive work, they might be able to narrow down their suspect pool to someone other than Mackenzie.

He was also still waiting for the lab reports to come back with DNA results from the glasses as well as the promised IP address for the computer from Oliver the tech. There just had to be something that would clear Mackenzie. Watching her on the interview, he just couldn't believe she'd done it. He only hoped he wasn't just wishfully thinking the best of her because he was attracted to her.

Chapter Twenty-Three

Dillion knocked on the detective's door, then opened it without waiting for a response.

"Sorry to bother you sir, but the tech sent over the IP address used by Lucas from Louise's computer." He thrust the information towards Caleb.

"Great."

"I think you'll find it surprising." Dillion added as he watched Caleb scan the papers.

Dillion was not disappointed when Caleb gasped, looking up in shock. "Is this right?"

"Yes, sir. Oliver said he checked it five time because he wanted to be absolutely positive in the results.

Caleb groaned. This was not going to go over well. Not at all. "What the hell am I supposed to do with this?" Caleb shook his head, then ran a hand through his hair. "Thanks Dillion. I'd better go talk to the Chief. Keep what you know under wraps."

Taking the report with him, Caleb headed up to

the chief's office. He felt absolutely ill. Stopping at the assistant's desk, he waited for Claire to finish her phone call, but with the receiver pressed against her ear, she looked up at him questioningly.

"Is she in?" he silently mouthed.

Claire nodded and Caleb walked past her to the wooden door, peeking in. Chief Beverly Hoffmeister looked up as Caleb came into view.

"Hey Caleb. Come on in. What's up?"

"A new development in the Harper Case." He handed her the tech's results.

"What exactly am I looking at?" She asked as she scanned the papers.

"The IP address and location for a suspect that she played games with on the computer."

Beverly's eyes widened when she realized who it implicated. She'd been keeping tabs on the case in general, but she never expected this result. "Talk about a small world." She set the papers on her desk, taping them with her fingers as she became lost in thought for a moment. "Who else knows?"

"The lab tech, Oliver, obviously, and Dillion

Davies who picked up the report. I've told him not to say anything."

"This is going to have to be handled with the utmost delicacy."

"Yeah. That's why I came to you first."

"What's the probability of this being the perp?"

"At this point, pretty high. Obviously, I've not had access to his computer to verify. Everything I obtained is from Louise's computer. However, it seems she'd figured out who it was and might've been black mailing him."

"Oh, that's just great." Beverly thought a bit more unconsciously drumming her long slender fingers once again. "We have to be smart about it."

"Yes, Ma'am." Caleb waited for his superior. He knew this information was potentially volatile in more ways than one.

"I'll call him in here, to my office. We'll conduct the interview together and in private."

Caleb nodded. It was a sound plan.

"Do you have everything you're going to need before he arrives?"

"Most of my files are downstairs. I'll go get them and have Dillion meet me back here. He can remain outside for security and to make sure this remains private until we see where it goes."

"You have ten minutes. As it turns out, I see a note from Claire that I have a meeting with him in ten minutes. Isn't that ironic and convenient?" Beverly followed Caleb out of the office only to stop at Claire's desk.

Caleb virtually ran to his office, located Dillion with instructions and took the stairs back up two at a time. He'd arrived at the chief's office just as his suspect did. He patiently stood aside while Mayor John Davis was welcomed by Beverly.

"John. Thanks for coming." Beverly smiled leading him to one of the two guest chairs in front of the large desk and taking a seat next to him.

She indicated Caleb was to take her seat behind the desk. He appreciated the advantage this gave him. John, however was slightly perplexed.

"I thought we had a meeting to discuss payroll. What's this about?"

Beverly spoke up. "Sorry, John. That was the original plan, but something has come up and we need to discuss it with you. Or rather Detective Mitchell does. I'm just an interested party who is also helping to protect your anonymity."

John frowned and stood up. "My anonymity? Whatever for? What are you talking about? I won't stand for these veiled insinuations. Let me know when you want to talk about the payroll." John started to head for the door when Dillion appeared, his arms crossed, blocking the doorway in a very stonewall manner. Sputtering, John turned around. "What's this about?"

"I'm sorry, Mayor, but I have some questions that need to be answered with regards to a case I'm working on. You can either answer them here, or Officer Davies can publicly escort you to interrogation."

"Please John." Beverly cajoled. "We can keep this more private if you just sit down here and answer the questions."

John hesitated slightly, but seeing the obstacle

Dillion was presenting, he decided to take the more acquiescing path and sat back down.

"Thank you." Caleb really didn't want to do this, but he had to find someone other than Mackenzie for a suspect if he was to prove her innocence. "Do you know Louise Harper?" He pulled out his notes as well as his notepad and pen to jot down the mayor's answers.

"Yes. I've known her for years."

"When's the last time you spoke or saw her?"

"Last time I saw her was probably a week or so ago. It's when my family and I were having dinner with the Channing Family at the Blue Ox. She stopped by the table and started a ruckus. Surprised me entirely. I didn't think she had that kind of a personality, but she really seemed overzealous with Tyler and overly obnoxious with the rest of his family, especially his wife, Debra."

"And the last time you spoke with her?"

John rubbed the back of his head as he thought about it. "I guess the same night as that incident. I don't believe I've seen or talked to her since."

"What about as Lucas Hardgrove?"

John paled slightly. "Who?"

Caleb sighed. He'd hoped the interview would go more smoothly but it'd be more difficult if John kept lying. He pulled the tech report and slid it across the desk. "According to the technical department, your computer is the IP address for Lucas Hardgrove, a role play character that played with Louise Harper who portrayed the character Lily Esystreet. With that information in hand, I also see that you last played and spoke to her the night of her murder, which was last Saturday."

John didn't say anything, just looked at the report he couldn't readily read all the technical jargon of.

Caleb pushed another set of papers across the desk to him. "These are copies of the chats and some of the threads between Lily and Lucas over the past couple of weeks. The threads are part of the game, which gets intensely intimate. The chats are a bit more telling, however."

John pushed them back. "I know about them.

I'd prefer not to read them though."

"Are you Lucas?"

John paused, looking nervously around the room, then settling on Caleb. "Yes. But I didn't kill Louise."

"Did she know you were Lucas?"

"I don't think so. At least not until a couple of weeks ago."

"What makes you think she found out then?"

"Because after the incident at the Blue Ox, she contacted me personally. Not on the Lucas account and told me she knew I was playing Lucas. She said if I didn't help her beat the charges and be able to continue to see Tyler Channing, she'd tell everyone about the role playing game."

"So, basically she was starting to blackmail you."

It was a statement, not a question, but John nodded his head slightly. He refused to look at Beverly.

"How do you think she found out you were Lucas?"

"I said something that was something I always say in chat when we played. It struck a chord in her to the point it clicked, I guess."

"When did you learn Louise was Lily?"

"For several months now. Almost from the beginning. She'd tell me all about her life, and it was obvious who she was talking about even if she didn't give her real name."

"Yet, knowing it was someone in your district, you continued to play with her?"

"Sure. She didn't know who I was and I got to live out my fantasies with her that my wife wouldn't even consider. And if Louise told my wife, as she threatened to do, or it got out to the community, I'd lose everything. Everything! Don't you see?"

"So, you killed her to keep her quiet."

"No. No. I couldn't do that. I admit, part of me was in love with her. She was broken because of being neglected by Al. I brought something into her life that gave her strength and purpose. Even if we weren't physically together, I was able to see her change, grow, become stronger. I can't tell you how thrilled I was when she took the initiative and threw that lazy son-of-a-bitch out the door and basically out of her life. She'd never have done that before we started role-playing. But, I also knew she wouldn't hurt me. She didn't ask for much. It wasn't like she wanted money or anything. She wanted time to spend in her fantasy world with the real face behind Lucas. Tyler Channing. We each got something out of it. I gave her strength and an escape from her boring life and she gave me sexual fantasy that I could disappear in, away from the real world." He sighed and looked at Beverly for the first time. "I suppose this will all come out in a glorious scandal?"

Caleb intervened with a question of his own. "Where were you Saturday night?"

John lowered his head before turning back to Caleb. "I saw Louise. I went to speak to her in person about ten that night. She was already dead."

Caleb frowned. "Why don't you start from the beginning and tell me everything. Don't leave anything out."

John looked around the room again, especially towards the door, which was now closed. He was sure Dillion was guarding it from any accidently coming in.

Beverly followed his eyes around the room, settling on the door. "No one will bother us. As I mentioned earlier, I wanted to keep this as much on the down-low as possible until we heard your side of things."

"I appreciate that very much, Beverly. I know this looks bad, but honestly, I didn't kill her."

"We're listening, John. Just tell Caleb your story. We'll do our best to keep this private as best we can."

Nodding slightly, John turned back to Caleb. "We talked on Wednesday. She contacted me and said she knew I was Lucas from a phrase she overheard when I was having dinner with the Channing's. As I said earlier. She told me she was Lily and she wanted help. She wanted to make sure I could find a loop-hole or something to prevent the

Order of Protection from going through. She wanted to be able to continue to see Tyler. She stated she had some news she wanted to share with him, something she hadn't told anyone, although she had eluded several times to Al not being Mackenzie's biological father.

She called me Saturday morning. Said that she tried to get into the theater to see Tyler and there was new security there. Also that she'd been served with an Order of Protection to stay away from the entire Channing family. She wanted help to get into the theater as well as remove the order somehow. I told her I'd look into it and see what I could do.

That's when she threatened me. She insinuated she'd tell everyone about us being together. She admitted she would exaggerate just to get her points across, but it wouldn't matter if everything she said wasn't the entire truth. It'd ruin me. My career and my family with just the hint of scandal. Everyone is always willing to believe the worse in people, especially in politicians. So, I told her I'd be over later that evening and we could discuss it. She said she'd leave the back door open for me so I could just sneak in without the neighbors seeing and becoming suspicious.

I got there about ten. The house was lit, but quiet and when I called out to her after I entered, there was no sound. I looked around the kitchen, then headed into the living room. That's when I saw her by the beverage cart. There was blood everywhere. I don't think I ever saw so much in real life as I did. I got a bit sick and threw up in the kitchen sink. I rinsed it, then grabbed one of those wet cleaning sheets and wiped down everything I touched. I headed into the room again, just to make sure she didn't have anything that might implicate me. I saw a stack of papers on the table and when I looked at them, I realized they were transcripts of our chats. There was already a fire burning in the fireplace, so I tossed the papers in there. I wasn't thinking about the computer. I wasn't thinking about anything really. I grabbed the poker and made sure the papers caught on fire, wiped the poker down and slipped out the way I came. I just wanted to get away from there and forget I ever saw all that blood. That's the truth. She was already dead."

"You do realize you just committed a class 4 felony? That's one to four years. Why didn't you call the police when you found her?"

John paled. "I know. I wasn't thinking anything other than I couldn't be there. No one could know I was at her place or why. And what was I supposed to say if I called the police? Why I was there? It would've defeated the whole purpose of going there secretively if I did that."

"Why didn't you call it in anonymously?"

"Honestly, I didn't think of it. I was too shaken up to think totally rationally. My only thought was to get away before anyone saw me."

Caleb leaned back in the chair and steepled his fingers, the tips of his two forefingers rocking against his chin in thought.

"Would you be willing to give us your fingerprints and DNA?"

"If it'll help clear me and keep this between us, yes. You can have whatever you want. I know I made a mistake tampering with any evidence, but isn't there some way to work this out without it becoming public?"

Beverly stood. "I think we can work something out depending on the results of the prints and DNA. As for now, I believe we have enough information, John. We'll keep this under wraps as best we can until we solve this case and if what you say is the truth, the entire truth, we will maintain your secret. As for breaking the law, you are the mayor and your political affluences can work to your benefit at this moment in time. But, John, I'll expect a favor down the road for keeping this quite. And I hope you're telling us everything."

John stood. "I swear, Bev. I've told you both the entirety about what occurred that night. I'll add though, I don't think Tyler is Mackenzie's father, but I don't think Al is either. I'm not sure if that has anything to do with Louise's death or not, but I thought I'd mention it."

Beverly showed John out and shut the door again so Caleb and she could talk privately. Caleb gathered his papers and moved around to the front of the desk, allowing Beverly to take her seat. "What do you think?"

"Truthfully? I think Mayor Davis is telling us everything. I think he's too frightened to hold anything back, knowing if he did, we might expose him and his entire life would be ruined. I know Mary Davis. She is not a mousy woman. If she thought for one second John was cheating on her, she'd have him in divorce court so fast his head would be spinning like the Exorcist. I've always thought he was a bit afraid of her. As such, I don't think he'd hold anything back. I also don't think he'd kill anyone. Even in anger. He seems to insipid to murder anyone, much less someone like Louise."

"I agree. I don't think he killed Louise. I believe him when he says he loved her. Even if it was a very bazaar relationship. If you can even call it that."

Caleb agreed. Although he wasn't too happy he wasn't any closer to finding out who was the murderer.

Chapter Twenty-Four

Byron stared at the phone. Ms. Marian had just stopped by with news that Mackenzie Harper had been arrested for the murder of her mother. She'd heard that from her niece Maggie. For some reason, Maggie seemed overly relieved to have the killer found and have the attention taken away from the Channing Family as well as herself. However, Byron was sure Mackenzie wasn't the killer. It just wasn't in her to hurt her mother. However, having inside information as to who the murderer was did help.

Although this was a pretty big city, there were pockets, especially in the theater community that everyone was close as if they lived in a small town instead. A world in and of itself, many have said over the years. And it was true. Not much happened in the theater world without the others knowing or finding out about it. Rumors abounded, but rumors always had a bit of truth to it. And he knew Ms. Marian knew the truth. Knew what he'd done. And she knew why. That made her as dangerous as Louise. Would anyone believe a 75-year-old? Would she even tell anyone? After all, she'd kept quiet thus far. Still he had to worry about the whole affair.

It didn't help that Ms. Marian was Maggie's aunt, or that Maggie was so involved with the Channing Family. It would've been so much easier if the whole lot of them were total strangers to Valley View.

But, he'd done this. He lined all the dominoes up, he should've been more prepared when they came tumbling down. The question was, should he give himself up? He figured the police would figure it out eventually, but why wait longer than necessary? Or did he really think he'd get away with it just because he had done so thus far? Should he just call them and have the whole thing over with? Or wait and hope they never figured it out? Still, he didn't want Mackenzie to go away for something he knew she didn't do.

Maybe he just needed to wait a bit longer and

let things work themselves out? Frustrated with his indecision, he threw his desk phone against the wall before storming out of the room.

CRIME SCENE DO NOT CROSS

Maggie hung up the phone with her aunt. The whole affair was tense. She could see the effect it was having on Tyler and Debra and she wished she could do more to protect them from the onslaught of everything.

Somehow, the death of Louise and her connection to Tyler leaked out. Considering Tyler's fame, it shouldn't be totally surprising, but yet, none of them expected it so soon. Maggie realized it was only because Debra had Louise arrested the night Tyler arrived. Add to that, the Order of Protection against Louise as well as the whole camera incident and it was only natural the papers caught on to the story.

Maggie had heard through the grapevine, Louise's daughter, Mackenzie had been arrested for her mother's murder. Maybe now the Channing's could get back to some form of normalcy. To her, that was good news. Her job was safe and the person she privately cared about could still remain close to her.

She knew there was no chance for her and the person she was in love with. She couldn't help being in love with them either, but when you spend so much time with one person, doing things for them, helping them, it just happens. Oh, Maggie knew her feelings wouldn't be reciprocated. And she wouldn't allow them to be anyways. She'd seen the hurt, disappointment, the pure struggle to hurt someone like that and she wouldn't be a part of it. She was fine hiding her feelings away. She was fine protecting her love and their family while hiding behind the mask of being an assistant. It was a job. One she would do anything for. One which allowed her to spend every day with the person of her dreams, even though nothing would come of it. One she would kill for in order to keep safe.

The door to the suite opened as Debra and Pearl came in carrying several bags, breaking her thoughts. They'd been shopping again. Both felt more at ease knowing they wouldn't be followed by Louise and her, now broken camera. It felt good to see them both relaxed and laughing easily showing off their new purchases.

"Your father called, Debra. He wanted to be sure you were all doing okay and he wanted to remind you he had no problem should you decide to divorce Tyler."

Debra laughed. "He's been telling me that since my wedding day nineteen years ago. I don't think he appreciated that I was pregnant before I got married. Even though we had talked about a wedding and it was mostly planned beforehand, we just upped the date so it wouldn't be quite so obvious."

"I have a feeling your father would be perfectly happy if you were never married. At least to an actor."

"Honestly, I don't think he would've approved of anyone. No one good enough for his girl." Debra set the bags on the couch. She still hadn't let Tyler back in her bed, but maybe it was time.

"Sounds like dad." Pearl mumbled. She would be glad to head off to college soon just to have some time away from her parents. She loved them dearly, but they could both be a bit overbearing sometimes, always wanting to protect her when she didn't feel like she needed their bubble-wrap protection.

"Do you need help with any of those?" Maggie asked.

"Do you have the time? If so, I could use some assistance." Debra replied.

"I'm fine. Mom, going to put my things away in my room. Are we still getting together for dinner?"

"Yes. I'll call you when we're ready to go." Debra pointed to the bags for Maggie to bring into her bedroom. Once the two of them were alone, she turned to Maggie. "Can you do a couple of things for me?"

"Sure, what do you need?"

"Well, as I'm sure you're aware, I've forced Tyler to sleep on the couch the past few nights. I was so angry with him over Louise and so furious with her in general. Hell, I could've killed her myself." She laughed nervously. "Anyway, now that she is actually gone, I'd like to have him back in my bed tonight. So, I was hoping you'd make it a bit more romantic for when we return from dinner?"

"Anything in particular?"

"Of course." Debra wasn't sure if Maggie had a romantic bone in her body, she always seemed so aloof, but then again, that was one of the things she liked about the woman. At least she didn't have to worry about her going after Tyler like she had his last assistant. It made having Maggie around so much more pleasurable. "I have some of those battery operated candles. About 50 of them, so if you can have them lit and spread about, that would be great. Get a bottle of champagne on ice. No, wait. We had the champagne here from the hotel, it was mediocre at best. Can you go to the liquor store? No, there won't be time."

"The hotel has a good wine selection. Much better than their champagne. I could pick something out from here?"

"That would be perfect. I'll trust you on choosing something good. Bill it to the room. Well, you know. Maybe some flowers would be nice too?"

"Do you want rose petals on the bed spread?"

"That would be good. Maybe have the fireplace lit?"

"I'll have maintenance stop by and get that ready for you. Do you have an idea of when you'll be returning?"

"Give us about three hours after we leave for dinner."

"What about Pearl?"

"I think she'll be glad to have some alone time tonight. You might want to head out as well, once everything is seen to."

"Maybe Pearl and I can go to a concert. I know a local band that is playing tonight she might like."

"Oh, could you take her? I'd be so grateful."

"Not a problem. I love spending time with Pearl and she's only got a few weeks left before she heads off to college. Then who knows when we'll see her?"

"I know. I can't believe she is so grown up or how fast time went by. Seems like just yesterday when I was giving birth, and here, nineteen years later, she's headed off to college." Debra sighed wistfully.

Maggie gave her a pat on her arm. "I'll make sure everything is in order for you and Tyler. I'll stop by Pearl's room and make sure she wants to spend time with me at this concert. I can pick her up from the restaurant after your meal."

"That sounds perfect. Thank you Maggie."

Chapter Twenty-Five

Caleb had just gotten the warrants in hand and was headed into the phone company to get the records for the cell phones of the suspects when his own phone rang. Finding a corner to speak a bit more privately, the caller ID indicated it was Officer Simon. "Hey, Mark. Find something?"

"Yeah. Davies and I spoke to a couple of the neighbors and a few of them stated Mackenzie Harper was on the front lawn having a shouting match with her mother about 8:15 or 8:30. Several also saw Mackenzie drive away immediately after."

"That's good." He tried to keep some of the enthusiasm out of his voice and be nonchalant, but he wasn't sure if it was working. Not that Mark would say anything to him about it.

"Yeah. And here's something else. A couple of them reported seeing another car in the vicinity shortly after Mackenzie left. We got the description and one even gave us a partial plate."

"Did you run it?"

"Of course. It came back to Enterprise Rentals."

From Mark's tone, Caleb knew he had more pertinent information. "And?"

"And the car is registered to Tyler Channing."

Well, that was a bit of a surprise, and the newest suspect had motive as well. "See if you can find Mr. Channing and bring him into the station for another discussion. I'm going to get these phone records and I'll be right there."

Two hours later and Caleb was finally entering the police station with a folder almost as thick as a book. Dillion was waiting for him in the foyer. "Caleb, Tyler is waiting for you in interrogation room five. I'm also expecting to get the fingerprints back any moment now. I had the lab put a rush on it. Since the guy is famous, they were more than willing to move the samples to the front of the line."

"Great work, Dillion. Let me know as soon as the results come in. As for Mr. Channing, let him stew a bit longer. I want to go through these reports a bit more thoroughly before I meet with him again."

"No problem, sir."

Caleb headed down to his office. He'd gotten a preliminary account of the locations for the cell phones of all his major suspects, and there were no shortages of those. Noting some points he wanted to be sure to make, he smiled as he read one of the location markers, double checking it against the phone number. Grabbing the sheet, he left the rest on his desk and headed directly to the holding cells. It didn't take him long to find Mackenzie sitting on the bed, her knees raised up to her chest, her arms wrapped around her knees, looking disillusioned and miserable. Her head popped up when she noticed Caleb outside her barred door. She wasn't sure what to say, but she knew he was obviously there for her. Did he find the evidence he needed to fully arrest her? Or did he get the verification he needed to know she was innocent and was going to set her free?

"Mackenzie? I'm sorry you had to go through this." He pulled out a set of keys and unlocked the door.

She didn't move other than to lift her head. "You're just doing your job. I understand."

"We got confirmation from your mother's neighbors that you were, indeed, arguing out on the front lawn and left about 8:30pm. I also retrieved your cell phone records, and the tower your cell phone pinged off from is in Moraine Valley, away from your mother's home at the time of her death. I'm really sorry." He shifted from one foot to the other, not remembering the last time he felt this uncomfortable. "You're free to go."

Slowly she stood, moving to stand in front of him. "Thank you. I know you had to do this. I shouldn't have lied about not seeing my mother Saturday. I should've been upfront about getting that bottle of wine. I don't know why I wasn't. I guess I was scared. Scared of being a suspect, scared you would think I did this." She looked up at him, her hazel eyes unwavering. "Scared you wouldn't want anything to do with me since my mother was killed."

He blinked, slightly confused. Did she just say what he thought she just said? "I thought you'd be angry with me for having you arrested. For not trusting you."

"How could I be angry with that when I gave you a reason not to trust me? I know I ruined any chance of anything that might have…" She paused, her cheeks flaming hot. "Forgive me."

She turned to leave the cramped cell, but he grabbed her wrist and let his hand slide down to caress her fingers. "Please don't go yet. I didn't think you'd even consider getting to know me after I had you arrested. Is there? I mean, could there be a chance? For us?"

"Really?" She seemed incredulous that he'd still be interested in her.

"Really. Maybe I can take you out to dinner? When this is all over?"

"How soon do you think that will be?"

"Soon. I have a really good suspect now. If I'm right, they either did it or know who did. How about Pescano's on Saturday? If you'd do me the honor of going out with me?"

She smiled and nodded. "Yes. I'd really like that."

He held up the paper in his hand from the cell phone company. "I already have your number and address, so I'll pick you up on Saturday about 7:30?"

"I'll...I'll see you then." Not being able to take the smile off her face, she let Caleb guide her to the exit doors of the police station. It was only as the cool air hit her face did she realize she was free from being accused of killing her mother. But then she had to wonder who Caleb had yet to interrogate. Who was responsible for her mother's death?

Chapter Twenty-Six

Caleb sat across from Tyler. "Have you been read your rights, Mr. Channing?"

"Yeah. When the cops picked me up."

Caleb noticed he was far more subdued than the last time he was here. He wasn't going to ask if Tyler wanted a lawyer if his Miranda Rights had been given. Without a lawyer, he might actually get some answers and was willing to push it as far as he could.

"You weren't exactly honest with me the last time we talked."

"Yeah? How so?"

"According to my file here, the officers were able to find a neighbor who spotted your rental car parked on the street in front of Louise's home. Louise was part of a neighborhood watch and they jot down the make, model and license plate of any vehicle they feel is suspicious. In this case, it implicates you. If you didn't see her yesterday, why were you at her house?"

The revelation seemed to deflate Tyler. That was the problem of neighborhood watches, they were too nosy for their own good when someone was just trying to remain hidden from the public eye. So much for being anonymous. "Fine. I was there. I wanted to tell her to stop bugging my family. That even if we were together all those years ago, time moved forward and so did I. I didn't love her. I didn't know her. I had a court order out against her and I wanted her to know, if she cared about me, like she said she did, then she needed to leave me alone. She was upsetting my family, which in turn, upset me. I also wanted to point out that part of loving someone meant that you wanted them to be happy and she wasn't making me happy. After our little talk, I departed. She was alive when I left. I swear that's the truth."

"What time were you there?"

"I got there about 6:30 and left at seven. I drove around a bit, then headed to the train yards I'd spotted on my first day here. I really was there all night, and she was alive when I left."

"Your car was seen after 8:30 near the Harper home, not earlier."

"That's not possible. I left way before then. I swear she was *alive* when I departed her place."

Taking out another folder, Caleb opened it up and pulled out the top sheet to show Tyler. "According to your cell phone records, your phone pinged near Louise Harper's house until eleven. Shortly thereafter, it shows up at the train yard where you made a seventeen-minute call to a New York number."

"That was my agent, I called. I wanted to know what would happen if I broke the theater contract and left the play. We had a long discussion about what my contract to the theater entailed."

"From what I learned from the theater director, you couldn't get out of your contract without dire penalties, including loss of work for the run of the play." At the look for surprise on Tyler's face, Caleb continued. "I had a nice long discussion with Byron Cassiday about your contract the other day."

"Fine. That's true. I'd've been in a precarious

situation if I chose to quit the production."

"So you went over to talk to Louise to tell her you wanted to stay, but she needed to stop stalking you?"

"No. I wouldn't have had to talk to my agent about leaving if I'd killed her. It would've been a bit redundant. Don't you think?"

"Then explain why your phone pinged at the closest tower near Mrs. Harper's home."

Tyler shifted uncomfortably in his chair, his eyes looking everywhere but at Caleb.

Raising an eyebrow, Caleb patiently waited until Tyler was ready to talk.

After several minutes of uncomfortable silence, Tyler turned to face Caleb head-on. "Please, don't tell anyone what I'm about to tell you. If Debra found out? Well, I'd hate to think of the consequences."

"I can't make that promise. It all depends on what it is you have to tell me, but I will promise you this: if I don't have to use the information, I won't."

Tyler shifted in his seat again, thinking about it

for an additional few moments. "Fine. After I left Louise, I found a liquor store nearby. I went in and bought a bottle of whiskey. Then I sat in the car for hours debating on drinking it. See, I was an alcoholic once. And a drug addict. I went cold turkey decades ago when I thought I was going to lose Debra. But the strain of Louise and her creating stories that hurt Debra, I just wanted to get lost in an alcoholic stupor. But after I bought it, I couldn't drink it. I kept thinking if I did, Debra would find out and then it really would be over between us. It was a mental battle I waged for hours on whether or not to drink it as I sat in the parking lot debating. I'm sure if you check the lot cameras you'll see I was sitting there for a good couple of hours. Please. Don't let Debra know I almost drank for the purpose of getting drunk. She has so much on her plate right now. I just couldn't do that to her."

Of all the confessions Caleb expected to hear, this wasn't one of them. "Alright, Tyler. Let me check it out. If what you say is true, there is no reason for me to tell anyone you were somewhere else other than the train yards that night."

Tyler physically relaxed as he smiled. "Thank you."

Caleb had Sally search for liquor stores near both the cell tower and the Harper residence. Sally pulled up a map of the area and narrowed the search to two that qualified as possible locations. She wrote both addresses and phone numbers down, handing the paper to Caleb, who then made the phone calls to see if he could get the videos from each location voluntarily. He was grateful they were both willing and would have copies ready for him to be picked up at his convenience. He had Sally call Mark Simon on the radio in order to swing by and pick up the copies.

Within the hour, Mark was at the station with two USB drives in hand. The first one didn't show Tyler or his rental car; the second was just as Tyler indicated. Inside, it showed Tyler purchasing a huge bottle of whiskey at 7:32pm and then sitting in the back corner of the parking lot for the next couple of hours. Although Tyler couldn't be seen clearly, it was noticeable that there was someone in the vehicle and they never got out again once they got in. The car pulled away about 11pm. There was no way Tyler could be the killer. So then who was? And why did the rental car show up at Louise's neighborhood at 8:30pm? Literally one hour after Tyler vacated the premises.

Perplexed, he was about to head back upstairs, when his phone rang. Leaning over his now-cluttered desk, Caleb answered. "Detective Mitchell."

"Hi," a slightly hesitant feminine voice replied. "Are you the detective working on the Louise Harper case?"

"Yes. May I ask who's calling?"

"Oh." A small nervous chuckle came through the receiver. "I'm Kendall Roberts. I mean Falcon. Sorry, I just got married a couple of weeks ago. Not used to the new last name just yet."

"Mrs. Falcon. Thank you for calling. I'm sorry I've not been in touch sooner. I knew you'd only recently returned from your honeymoon." Caleb shifted back around his desk, returning to his seat.

"I wanted to let you know that I might have some information for you regarding Louise."

"I appreciate you calling. Any tip is helpful in tracking down Mrs. Harper's killer."

"She was a friend of mine. I don't have any family left and she sort of took me under her wing when I met her about a year ago. We became good friends and I just want her murderer brought to justice. That's why I had to call."

"I appreciate that. And your news?"

"Well, I was visiting the theater the other day. I ran into one of the Channing women. I'm sorry, I'm not sure her first name, but she asked me if I knew where Louise lived. Of course, I wouldn't tell her. That's private information. But she begged me, saying that Louise has been bothering the family and she wanted to talk to her and see if she could straighten out their issues, woman to woman. I think I did something wrong at this point."

"What did you do?"

"Well, I wouldn't give her Louise's address,

but I figured it wouldn't hurt to give her her phone number. Then if Louise wanted to see her, she could make her own arrangements. I just didn't think, I mean, how could I have known?" Kendall started to sob on the phone.

"Mrs. Falcon. You didn't know, and you only did what you thought was going to help. Letting me know is important knowledge and I appreciate you calling me today with this information."

Between the sniffles, Kendall responded, "You're welcome," disconnecting the phone call immediately after.

Caleb pulled out the phone tower location list and skimmed the information, finding one that matched. And not surprisingly, they had access to a second rental car that was also in Tyler Channing's name.

Chapter Twenty-Seven

Before he left the station, Sally called to him. "Sir, there is a Byron Cassiday in the lobby wanting to speak with you."

Puzzled, Caleb hated to put off his arrest at such a crucial moment. Still, Byron Cassiday might have some important news he needed to tie up any loose ends. "Tell Mark and Dillion to meet me but not go in. I'll be up to see Byron in a minute."

This so wasn't a good time, but he couldn't risk not getting all the information he could. He took the stairs two at a time, greeted Byron in the lobby and showed him to the interrogation room.

"Mr. Cassiday. You've kind of caught me at a bad time. How can I help you?"

"It's how I can help you, Detective. I know who the murderer is."

Oh, this should be good. "And who is that?"

"Maggie Keeler."

Catching his interest, Caleb pulled out his notepad and pen. "Why do you think it's Ms.

Keeler?"

"'Cause she's in love with Debra and wants to protect her."

"And you know this, how?"

"From a combination of Ms. Marian and Louise herself."

"What did they each say?"

"Ms. Marian told me about Maggie being in love with Debra and that she'd do anything for her. She said how much she hated what Louise was doing to upset her so much and that she was going to take care of it so Louise wouldn't bother them anymore. At first I thought it was with regards to the Order of Protection, but then after Louise was found dead, I figured she meant otherwise."

"And what did Louise tell you?"

"She was upset with me because I told her to leave Tyler alone. She thought telling me that Tyler was Mackenzie's father, that it would make a difference. I told her it wouldn't, because Tyler wasn't Mackenzie's father. I was and she needed to back down from bothering Tyler or he'd leave and

I'd be without a show."

"Why did you tell Louise you were Mackenzie's father? Is that true?"

"Yes. When Tyler was in Valley View for *The Hoosier Schoolmaster*, I too was on the production team. I knew both of them. I was younger, didn't have the beer belly I have now. Or the gray hair. People used to say I reminded them of Tyler in looks. Was just as handsome. Same intense hazel eyes and dark blond hair. But Tyler was always intoxicated from one thing or another. He'd sleep with every girl that would have him that caught his eye, but never the same one twice. Louise wanted to be with him, even then, but when she realized she didn't stand a chance, she turned to me. I think in her mind, because I looked a bit like Tyler, she felt she was with Tyler. For two weeks we were together every night. Then the play was canceled and Tyler headed back to Hollywood. With him gone, Louise ended it with me, but she was pregnant. She never came to me about it, so I never said anything—until Saturday night when I saw her.

I went to her place to tell her what happened, but then I saw the rental car used by Maggie down the street near Louise's house. I didn't want to bother them, figuring I'd come back later, but by then it was too late."

Caleb scribbled away madly, trying to keep up with everything Byron was telling him. "Why are you just coming forward now?"

"I didn't want you to accuse my daughter of killing her mother when I know she didn't do it. Maggie did."

"I wish you would've said something sooner, but I appreciate you coming forward now. Thank you." Caleb stood and quickly led Byron out so he could race to meet up with Mark and Dillion, who were waiting for him.

Chapter Twenty-Eight

With Mark and Dillion flanking either side of him, Caleb knocked forcefully on the penthouse suite of the Pennington Hotel. In his hand he held the warrant he'd obtained just thirty minutes ago. He'd already given a heads up to both officers on how to play it. Because all the accusations at this point were more-or-less circumstantial, the warrant was for one specific person while the evidence pointed to someone different. They'd make some tactical chess moves in order to get the killer to confess, or arrest the person on the warrant and know they got the right person after all.

Maggie opened the door and quickly stepped back when she realized the law was on the threshold. Caleb thrust the warrant at Maggie, spotting Debra on the couch reading while Pearl sat next to her watching television. Both looked up at the sudden intrusion, Debra setting her book aside and standing.

"What's this all about?" she inquired testily.

"It's about you lying to us, Mrs. Channing. And as a result, you're under arrest for the murder of Louise Harper."

"How? How did I lie to you?"

"Do you really want to do this here?" Caleb asked, as he nodded back to Mark and Dillion. "We have a warrant to search the suite."

Mark and Dillion began rummaging around the rooms while Maggie stood by the door as Debra and Pearl remained near the couch.

"According to the neighbors reports, a rental vehicle was seen in the vicinity of Louise's home on the night of her murder. Actually, two of them were, but we've accounted for the one utilized by Tyler as being there earlier. We have since confirmed where he was after he left. However, when we continued to investigate the details, we realized Mr. Channing had rented two cars, which means you were using the other. According to your phone records, you were near the residence upon the time of her death. You have opportunity and motive. On top of that, we learned from a reliable source that you asked for Louise's address the day of her demise."

"I didn't ask for her address and I didn't use the vehicle that night. I was in the park near her house speaking with Dr. Knox, our marriage counselor, and then with my lawyer, Jon Fernstein. Surely, my cell phone records indicated I was on the phone during that time. How could I kill her and still be talking on the phone?"

"There is enough down time between the phone calls that you could've committed the murder."

"But it wasn't me. I didn't..." Debra's eyes widened and she glanced at Pearl, then Maggie, before turning back to Caleb. "You caught me. I hated that Louise was stalking my family. I went over there to put an end to her insinuations once and for all."

Caleb frowned, crossing his arms as he narrowed his eyes. "So you went over there to shoot her?"

"Yes. Yes, I did it." Debra lowered her head in shame.

"No. Wait. I did it. I killed Louise," Maggie stepped up. She looked at Debra, a deep concern in her eyes. "I hated seeing what she was doing to the Channing family. I went over to talk to her after dinner with my family. I just had to see if I could help. Somehow. Debra is innocent. I shot Louise." She turned to face Debra. "I'm sorry. I was only doing what I thought would help."

"Why do you think lying would help Debra?"

"I wasn't lying. I am trying to tell the truth. I don't want Debra to go to prison for my crime."

Caleb sighed. First he had no suspects and now he had too many. Thing was, he knew both of the women were lying.

"Louise wasn't shot. And you just said you didn't have the car that night." He turned to Maggie. "You're saying you killed Louise? Yet that's impossible. Because Louise wasn't shot." He raised his eyebrow questioningly, knowing better than to believe her.

"Um." Maggie looked at Debra, then lowered her eyes. She realized she shouldn't have spoken too soon in defense of Debra.

"That's what I thought. I understand your loyalty, Maggie, but this is a serious matter." He looked over at Pearl, who was sitting quietly on the couch. He watched as she turned off the television set that she had muted earlier before he continued. "The thing is, I think you both realize who is left to be the killer. Someone who had free time. Someone who had access to the car. Someone whose cell phone was close enough to read from several towers near Louise's home. Someone like…?" Caleb had a feeling he didn't need to name who he was sure the murderer was. And he was right.

"I did it. Mom and Maggie are just trying to cover for me." Pearl stood. "Louise wasn't shot, she was stabbed."

"With what?"

"A corkscrew."

Caleb then knew he had the right person for the murder. "Pearl Channing, you are under arrest. Turn around and put your hands behind your head."

Pearl followed the instructions as Debra tried to

deny her daughter committed the deed. "Wait. This can't be. Why would she do it? She barely had anything to do with Louise."

"No, Mom. I did it. I did it for you and Dad. Earlier, I found some papers and pictures in Dad's trash in his dressing room. I knew she had proof that I had a half-sister, and I knew if she came out with this information, it'd make things worse between you two. I didn't want you to get a divorce over something stupid like what Dad did before you two met. I didn't want to be another statistic on the Hollywood couples scene.

"I'm the one who asked the author of the play where Louise lived. She wouldn't give me the address, but she did give me the phone number. After Mom and I split up, I called Louise and asked if I could see her to talk. She agreed and gave me the address. If you look at my phone's GPS, you'll see I have her coordinates on it.

Louise invited me in. We had some wine and cheese. I showed her the pictures and papers I found. She told me those were mostly copies and showed me the originals. I could see from the pictures of her daughter how much we looked alike, especially when we were younger. I knew, if Dad or Mom saw her kid, they'd see the resemblance as well. I couldn't have her destroy our family like that. I just couldn't. When she refused to keep it quiet, I lost it. I grabbed the corkscrew and just kept hitting her with it. I didn't even realize what I'd done until it was too late. I then took all the pictures and papers and burned them in the fireplace. I wiped anything I touched and left. I had my phone off during the entire time, so you probably couldn't tell where I was. Mom's innocent." Pearl looked over at her mom. "I'm sorry, Mom."

Debra had tears flowing down her face. "Don't you worry, baby. I'm going to have the best lawyers here for you. You're not going to be alone in this."

Mark confiscated Pearl's cell phone while Dillion came out of the room holding up a dress stained with blood he'd found in the bottom of the laundry pile. Caleb escorted Pearl towards the door. "Mrs. Channing, you can meet us at the station."

Caleb reached into his coat pocket and pulled out a card reading Pearl's Miranda Rights. "Pearl, you have the right to remain silent. Anything you say can and will be used against you in a court of law. You have the right to an attorney. If you cannot afford one, one will be appointed to you. Do you understand these rights as I've read them to you?"

"Yes, sir," Pearl said quietly as she was led out of the suite, nervous as to what would happen to her now.

Epilogue

Tyler held Debra's hand tightly as the judge passed sentencing on their daughter, Pearl. The jury found her guilty of manslaughter, realizing Pearl hadn't planned on visiting Louise with the intent to kill her, but it happened in a fit of rage.

As the courtroom emptied out, Tyler turned to see a young woman staring at him with his eyes and knew from the proceedings the woman was Mackenzie, his daughter with Louise. Beside her was Caleb, who had his arm wrapped around her shoulders for support. Tyler knew Mackenzie wouldn't approach him. She'd had plenty of chances before and hadn't. Squeezing Debra's hand, he let her go and moved to stand in front of Mackenzie, starring at her quietly for a few minutes.

"I know this is a bit awkward. I'm sorry about what happened to your mother."

"Thank you." Mackenzie forced a weak smile, unsure what more to say.

"I heard the results of the DNA test says your

mother was right in stating I'm your father."

"That's correct. But then, you're never going to be my dad. I don't mean that as an insult. I hope you understand."

"I do. It makes sense. The man you know as your dad is the one who raised you. I didn't have the chance. I didn't know about you."

"I know you didn't. Mom kept that pretty secret." She shifted uncomfortably.

"I'd like the chance to get to know you better, though. I understand I can't be your dad right away, but it's not like I don't want to be a part of your life."

"I'd like that, but aren't you going back to California soon?"

Debra shook her head as she approached the small group. "No. We are moving here. Our daughter is here, and we won't leave her just because of a mistake she made."

"Mistake? Is that what you think she did when she took a life?"

Tyler spoke up immediately. "I'm sorry. That's

not what Debra meant. She just means…we won't abandon our daughter to remain in this part of the country by herself as she serves her sentence. And I don't want to abandon you either. I'd really like to get to know you, if you don't feel it's too late for us."

Mackenzie was silent for a bit, her gaze shifting between the two of them. "I guess I can understand and appreciate that you don't want to leave Pearl here while you go on with your lives in California. And I would like to get to know you better. As my father."

"Thank you." Tyler handed her a piece of paper. "My phone number. Call me next week and we can set up a lunch or coffee or something."

Mackenzie took the paper and tucked it into her purse. "I will."

She watched as the two of them left the court room, hand in hand, feeling bad about the whole thing and wondering what her mother would think now that they were going to try and build a relationship where none had existed before.

When the proceedings for the trial began, Byron approached her to say he was her father. That he'd dated Louise while Tyler was in town twenty-three years ago. That Tyler would have nothing to do with her. So to prove it, they took a paternity test. It was a complete surprise when it came back negative. Caleb then asked both Al and Tyler if they'd be willing to end the question of fatherhood and both agreed.

Tyler still didn't remember any time they'd spent together and, from Byron's account, it might have only been one time. Probably before she got together with Byron. Al was just the man to make Louise's pregnancy legit. Such a mess. Thinking about the whole thing gave Mackenzie a headache. However, she smiled as she felt a warm hand at the small of her back.

"Are you okay?" Caleb asked softly.

"No. But I will be. It's going to take time." She leaned into him, letting him wrap an arm about her waist. They'd been out on several dates over the past couple of months. Mackenzie truly appreciated how he hadn't pushed her in any way, yet was a solid rock of support. She was sure she wouldn't have gotten through the ordeal, much less the trial, without him by her side.

As they stood on top of the courthouse steps, she turned to him. "Have I thanked you recently for everything you've done?"

"No thanks are necessary, babe. I'll always be here for you."

She leaned over and kissed him deeply. "I know."

ABOUT THE AUTHOR

Ms. Hawks has always been interested in writing in some form or other, including writing for a local newspaper. Deciding to become more knowledgeable, she headed back to school and received her Master's Degree in Ancient Civilizations, Native American History and United States History.

It was at this time she got involved in role playing on FaceBook, which gave her ample opportunities to grow and hone her writing ability.

She lives in the suburbs of Chicago with her four companions, all males... cats. She travels as much as she can to various Author/Reader conventions and loves to meet established fans and make new ones, some of which she considers friends more than fans. Check out her social media sites to follow her.

WebSite: AuthorLauraHawks.com
Twitter: AuthorLHawks
FB Author page:
https://www.facebook.com/LauraHawks-249262585192270/?fref=ts
FB Fan Group: Hawks Flock:
https://www.facebook.com/groups

MORE FROM LAURA HAWKS

Valley View Mysteries
Contemporary Suspense/Thriller

LAURA HAWKS

FLAMING
RETRIBUTION

Demon Trilogy

DEMON'S DREAM

LAURA HAWKS

Spirit Walker's Saga

Paranormal Ghosts

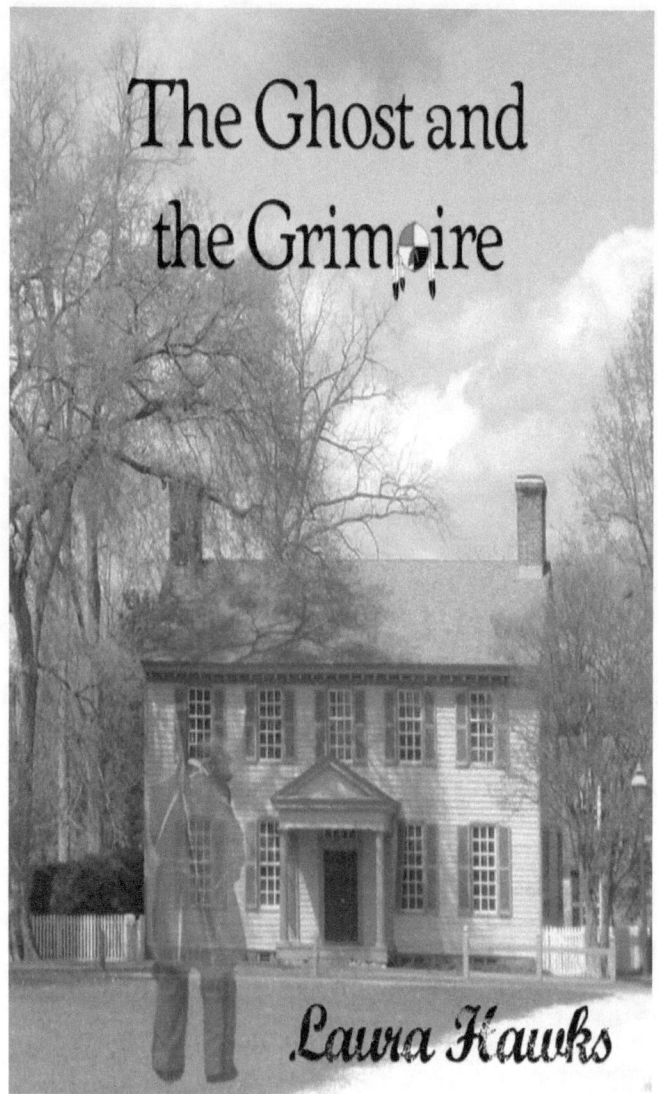

The Ghost and
the Grimoire

Laura Hawks

Shatter Fairytales

Laura Hawks

Snow White
and the
Seven Cannibals

Paranormal Romantic Mystery

EGYPTIAN DESTINY
THE WEIGHT OF HER FEATHER

LAURA HAWKS

Paranormal YA Mystery

Gumshoe
AND THE
MYSTERIOUS MUSHROOMS

LAURA HAWKS